# AFGHAN
## Camel Strings and the Australian Outback

# AFGHAN
## Camel Strings and the Australian Outback

Nigel Clayton

First Published in Australia by
Meni Publishing and Binding in 2008
Copyright © Nigel Clayton, 2008
This edition: Zuytdorp Press, 2022

The original National Library of Australia Cataloguing-in-
Publication data:
Afghan – Camel Strings and the Australian Outback, 1st ed.
1. Cameleers – Australia – Fiction. 2. Afghans – Australia –
History – Fiction.
A823.4

ISBN 978 0 6454632 4 8

BISAC

DRA012000    DRAMA / Australian & Oceanian
FIC014000    FICTION / Historical / General
FIC002000    FICTION / Action & Adventure

Poetry/story book - Children

A Pygmy Possum Named Henry
A Turtle Named Myrtle
A Crow Named Wahn
A Girl Named Castor

Adult poetry by this author:

Afghan - Song of the Desert
Orcinus Orca - Song of the Ocean
Hollandia Nova - Song of the Coast
Kibeho - An Epic Poem
Song of the Templar
Songs of Australia - A Poetic Trilogy
1453 - Constantinople

Other Titles

The Long Road to Rwanda
The Templar: and the City of God [Part 1]
The Templar: and the Temple of Káros [Part 2]
The Templar: and the Cross of Christ [Part 3]
Amazon [Part 4 of The Templar series]
Chivalry [Omnibus]
Underworld
Templar, Assassination, Trial & Torture
Dreamtime - An Aboriginal Odyssey
This Pestilence, Bergen-Belsen
When the Virgin Falls
Colonies of Earth [Also known as Mildratawa]
Fall of the Inca Empire
The Kibeho Massacre: As It Happened
The Zuytdorp Survivors
Tom of Twofold Bay
Afghan - The Script
Kibeho - Original Script

## CHAPTER ONE

Hergott Springs became known as Marree on 20th Dec, 1883, a town replacing the nearby settlement in name and commodity.

Its growth from its humble beginnings as a maintenance camp for the overland telegraph line could easily have been expected, and in particular for its growth in ethnic population; along with the nickname 'Little Asia'. Its populace of Afghan camel handlers was well known and could hardly be missed, raised from fledgling wings to portray a growing aspect of Australian society where sixty Afghan cameleers and their families maintained a thriving business... and sometimes it wasn't so thriving.

The cameleers would work for a quarter of what a white man would work, hence the white Australian falling cursed victim to the dark traders-of-the-desert, not to mention the fact that the white mans' bullocks and horses were no match for the single-humped camel, the dromedaries.

The cameleers weren't just from Afghanistan, even if collectively known as Afghans, but from a wide range of ethnic backgrounds; from Kashmir, Punjab, Baluchistan [Balochistan], Sind, Persia, Egypt and Turkey. Costs for cartage via camel were favourable to all. Camels ate the bush of the desert and needed little other supplement and could go so much longer without water when compared to a horse; and above all else, horses needed to be shod.

With the assent of the government to continue with the building of the railroad came an influx of activity to Marree;

Marree was now an endowed part of the heritage towards the growing strides of a great nation and served well those settlements, homesteads and farmers, and whoever else might be in need of supplies and assistance, along the Birdsville, Strzelecki and Oodnadatta Tracks, not to mention the paths trodden hard by camel strings to other places upon the map such as Broken Hill, Alice Springs, Coolgardie and Innamincka. The entire area for hundreds of miles around was ruled by floods, prolonged droughts and sandstorms; all of which were certain upheavals for the settlers – the colonists who relied upon 'on-time' delivery of supplies and a method by which to get their merchandise to purchasers as quickly as possible.

There was a police station here which was manned by three men of uniform, a general store and a post office; somewhat of a formal arrangement in the process of being recognized as a dot on a map; but for the people that lived and worked out of this town in the middle of nowhere, it was a spectacle of judgement and life. One other aspect which concerns the people of any town, regardless of size, was the final resting place for those that had met with death, and it was the cemetery that showed likeness to prejudice and naivety, for it was split into three parts; Aboriginal, Afghan and white.

Marree was derived from an Aboriginal word meaning 'many possums', but how times change the face value of a place such as this, where possums may have once been in vast numbers: now in Marree, 1884, there exist over 1,500 camels and a mosque in which the cameleers could give praise during certain times of the day, a mosque surrounded by date palms and a system by which to draw from flowing water in order to carry out ablutions prior to prayer.

The bush, as was found around the town of Marree, was a hot place not to be reckoned with, an inhospitable place for many, if not most, with its seemingly natural infestation of flies and ants which were simply too numerous to count or waste time worrying about, pests of the world which doused every inch of land from here to Timbuktu, and in the scorching heat which was a replica of the days and weeks before, varying only slightly from one day to the next, anything from 40 to 52 degrees in the shade having to be put up with. It was the calling of the desert: hot by day and cold by night.

Christmas day was just concluded, not that there were any Christmas trees or decorations to be seen, and business for the inhabitants continued as always, where men, horses, camels and bullocks could be found in strings and pulling wagons of many sizes; and the telegraph line was planted, stretching its way north towards Darwin from Port Augusta, from August 1870 to July 1872.

## CHAPTER TWO

Nak Kadir was 42 and looked long in the tooth, literally. His gums were well parted from the teeth and they neither glistened nor appeared to be looked after. Stained brown beyond belief, as with most cameleers, the mouth of teeth announcing their presence to the world, huge and almost bare to their roots. He wasn't smiling; his lips were seemingly held back from joining, as though an invisible barrier separated the upper lip from the lower, appearing more like a permanent grimace than anything else, scar tissue evident. He was set apart from all those that he knew, no other adorning the features which he displayed for the world to see, an uncontrollable fact about his character that he could have done well without.

He'd been standing at the gateway to Marree for some time, all morning in fact, awaiting the arrival of a particular person, a man of desperate measures that had left his home in the hills of Afghanistan to find his fortune in Australia, to ward off the countries sinful ways and to wrap himself around great reward and earning great praise from his family back home. Nak was awaiting the arrival of Abdul Hassan, a young man of just 23 years of age who had found himself with a wife and two children in this early stage of his life.

Nak surveyed the line up and down, a white turban upon his head needing a good clean, the robes that he wore more in tune to a robe that a rich man wore after dinner and prior to going to bed, clothing that was common but not altogether convenient in times when there was work to be done.

For the most part he didn't have a head for losing self-control, neither did he have a great amount of patience, and the time of day was starting to get the better of him. The train should have arrived some time ago and yet there was still nothing to be seen or heard. If the train was running late then surely a message would have been cast upon him via the telegraph line which hung over the town.

The Muslim men were quite exotic when compared to the Europeans, whether viewing them from Marree, further north, or further south. Anywhere upon the dry and barren surrounds of the very heart of Australia could be found an Afghan and a string of camels.

The Afghans were first brought into the country in vast number during the 1860s along with their camels; it was an introduction that was well suited to the desert terrain of the interior, much more so than the bullock or the horse, but this didn't detract from the fact that eighteen Afghans arrived in South Australia in 1838, a long and lengthy process then being suffered between the years before the trading of camels between nations really began.

Transportation between settlements and the like in the outback relied heavily upon the ability to deliver on time and with little sacrifice, considerations that could not be filled appropriately by the bullock or horse, let alone the men that served to drive them. The men of European cast were as unsuccessful as the animals which they worked and nowhere near as hardy and strong as the cameleers. The very determination within these exotic men was unbelievable and simply couldn't compare to anyone with white skin. Colonists were apt to fall jealous of those that served the settlements and interior, turbans wrapped around heads full of independence.

There existed little understanding of the Afghan in most places, in particular the settlements and homesteads so far from civilization. The further away you travelled from a major bustling city the more misunderstanding there was and quite often, more than not, they were feared for what so little was known about them.

Along the Birdsville Track, which lead to its namesake being changed from Diamantina Crossing to Birdsville, there were many small stations and homesteads such as Lake Harry Homestead, Mulka Homestead, Planet Downs, Alton Downs, and many others that spread far and wide, not to forget Pandie Pandie which was just over nine miles south of the Queensland border and nearer the destination of Nak and his crew than Birdsville itself. Birdsville was little more than a service centre for the pastoral properties that were sparsely fitted into the terrain like ore deposits spread across a barren landscape, but the Afghans were men all the same, more so than others, here in this country to serve the settlers, to carry on in business in order to make a living and in most cases to send money home to their families which were living hard lives. And the hatred for them grew in some places to the extreme where unnecessary actions were carried out upon them, simply because they were different. The Afghans were here to make their fortune, a fortune which eluded the vast majority for wages were trimmed in order to maintain a steady flow of employment; the colonists on the other hand, in particular those spreading their fledgling wings both far and wide, were in the race for pastoral land, a great land-grab in a harsh environment.

It was then that he heard it, saw the glimmer of hope reveal itself to him and the world. The train was inbound and the new man, Abdul Hassan, would be set upon his work without a shadow of a doubt. All men wishing to embark upon the lonely voyage to Australia in order to seek his fortune were considered a keen cameleer, and those that weren't would soon learn the ways of a camel handler as though born to it.

Nak then drew upon the common knowledge that he knew so well, that money in the pocket and work to be had was not always available... some more than the other and at other times hard to come by entirely.

Nak had received confirmation that a job was awaiting him and it was his great partner and friend, Shir Adji: 33 years old who was as ugly as a camel's backside - spoken politely, that was currently tending to the orchestrating of the supplies which they were to transport to a small homestead south of Birdsville.

Birdsville was a settlement of meagre worth, being fitted with three stores, a chemist, butchers shop, two hotels, a police station of almost dilapidated state and a blacksmith, the latter offering little to no advantage to cameleers for the camels didn't require shoes as did horses.

The small pastoral property south of Birdsville and Pandie Pandie also wished for their wool to be brought back to Marree and deposited upon the first available train to Port Augusta where the load would be picked up by a white man before continuing its journey on towards Adelaide: as for why they required such a vast range of extensive supplies for, as ordered, was bewildering: possibly expansion or simply to sell for a profit to others in the area: Nak was not there to question, but to make a profit himself via the delivery to them and then the delivery of wool to train.

Shir was a reliable man, as honest as the day was long, but far too desperate to find himself an Afghan wife, a matter which was to Nak's disappointment, for an arranged marriage was to unfold this night, the last night to be spent in Marree for quite some time, for the trek to Birdsville would commence on the morrow.

Nak needed Abdul as much as Shir in order to remain in good favour with those that he'd promised to provide assistance to, whether it be the arrival of supplies or the delivery of their wool and other merchandise to the railway terminal in Marree. One lost job could mean all the difference between survival and damnation, all the more prevalent with the threat of Faiz Mahomet hanging over his head, a forwarding agent and general carrier who employed many men and ran a profitable business from Marree. Faiz was a jemadar many years before, over five hundred men working beneath him on the Karachi wharves. He was well respected and seemingly favoured by Allah.

He pondered the life which was to befall Abdul as the train approached, thinking hard on what the young man had in store for himself, the dilapidated surrounds, the Ghantown that he had come to know and trust, where homes were built of the cheapest and most insufficient commodities that there was to offer and where corrugated iron roofs sheltered them from the rain during the onset of the rainy season. Even the mosque in which he attended was little different, but it's scanty look and appeal had no effect on the way in which they prayed, Muslims one and all.

The road beside the railway was busy, its hardened surface as good an indication as any to the traffic that travelled this way, countless hooves having contributed to the compacted ground, and the display of exuberance at present, from other men going about their daily business, did not distract Nak's frame of thought.

Nak looked at the railway track and then this road again, most briefly, as the train drew nearer, seeing another string of camels of Faiz Mahomet's entourage in business assets and interests going by, one cameleer to every ten camels, a little more than what Nak would like to undertake himself; it was normal practise for a single cameleer to handle up to eight camels and little more than that, but all depended, naturally enough, on the availability of good hands and the requirements for delivery.

There was much work in looking after a string of camels, much hard labour and foot slogging over beastly terrain, few luxuries and even fewer faces between post and settlement to ever be seen. It was a lonely life but one that was essential if Nak was to make a name for himself, to carve out a reasonably comfortable life for himself in his time of retirement from the endless days of tracking across the deserts along the same old land which he had traipsed before.

He brushed away more flies from his face, his skin dark brown and seemingly caked in dirt, though his skin was representative of many hours spent in the scorching Australian sun as it beat down without remorse.

## CHAPTER THREE

As the train's brakes filled the air with their methodical screeching, the stresses of the joints, engine and moving parts screaming out to all around, heads could be seen looking out upon him from within the window frames, mostly men with hard faces, creases cut deep in their flesh indicating many hours of hard labour and for little reward.

The engine and a single carriage had passed him before the train slowed sufficiently, and then in the doorway of the last carriage he saw a man of lean build and relative height catching his eye, as each passed before the train came to a full stop.

The man was handsome and wore a turban upon his head, pantaloon trousers that were dark in colour and tucked into high boots, a white shirt with a few stains here and there, with the sleeves pulled down to the wrist. The smile upon the man's face would have been contagious and spread to Nak, if it hadn't been for the fact that Nak's grimace was a perpetual stain upon his character, neither wishing to be moved nor removable by force: many men had tried but so seldom was there a fight to attend that Nak couldn't remember the last time he'd been hit hard in the face; even here in Marree, where the main persons of the bush were segregated by colour and creed. Here in Marree they all lived in relative harmony, each and every one of them understanding his and her place that had been created from the sand and the vastness of space surrounding them: despite the fact that the cameleers had to put up with constant, ethnic abuses, for they swallowed their pride in more case than not.

The man stepped down from the carriage.

"Are you Abdul Hassan?" asked Nak.

"Yes," he answered with the smile still in place, "I'm Abdul."

"I'm Nak Kadir. Do you have many things with you?"

"No," answered Abdul, his smile dissipating slightly but still turned up at the corners. "I have nothing with me."

"Nothing at all?"

"No."

"Do you have a sleeping blanket?"

"No."

"Spare clothes?"

"No."

"An empty sack in which to carry things, perhaps?"

"I have nothing to carry," replied Abdul. "I'm burden free. I have nothing but the goodness within me. I'm a hard worker and ready to work for you as though you were my own father."

Nak put his hand out and they both shook in acknowledgement of the bond which was to develop between them.

"Come with me," said Nak. "I'll take you to see Shir Adji. He's been my friend for as long as I've been in Hergott."

Abdul thought he'd made a mistake for a moment, reflecting on what he'd learnt from the time he'd purchased a ticket at the office back in Port Augusta, and the short stopover at the stations between there and where he was now, in particular Farina which he remembered well. This place looked so... isolated.

"I see the flies are as friendly here as they are anywhere else," said Abdul, his smile replenished.

Nak looked at him as they walked, unsure whether or not the new man was being sarcastic of the place which was to become his home between jobs, or if he was sincerely unrelenting in his good manner which was part and parcel of who he was.

"You'll get used to them even if they drive you crazy."

"I've heard that work is good here," offered Abdul of an opportunity to provide further conversation.

"It's good so long as you work without rest, beat your rivals in competition, and don't mind working for little more than what is needed in order to survive."

"But better than Afghanistan," stated Abdul. "The office in which I subscribed said that both work and money was fruitful and ready for the picking."

"You have to know the ropes, Abdul, or you will be taken advantage of," answered Nak. "Don't worry; you're in good hands with me. We are a private enterprise and don't work for those that are keen to take our contracts of employment. You must stay with me, Abdul, and stay away from those willing to rip the shirt from your back. Stay away from men like Faiz Mahomet or you will soon drown in your own sorrows."

"I will, Nak. When is our first job?"

"We'll depart tomorrow morning for a homestead near Birdsville. Sometimes it's better to move by night, especially in this heat and during Ramadan, but we'll travel by day. There'll be plenty for you to see."

"So you are from Kandahar?"

"Yes," answered Abdul.

"Good," said Nak. "I am from Kabul and Shir is from Karachi.

"Did you leave Afghanistan before the British moved in, or after?"

"After," said Nak, his voice indicating a little unsteadiness. "I fought in action against the British for two years and came here to Australia just over four years ago."

"And now you serve them."

Nak stopped temporarily in his tracks, "I serve no one," said Nak, "except me and my ambition. I will not be a servant to the British but must seize my better judgement in order to live a free life in the years to come. Though we are all prisoners in some small way, Abdul. I have higher ambition than to serve the unworthy. It's not for us to be treated unkindly for the good work that we do, but we always go unrewarded, without recognition, and are looked upon as though we are peasants."

"I was a tribesman back home," said Abdul.

"A tribesman isn't a peasant and nor should he be treated as such. Almost everyone in Afghanistan is treated the same, but more, more than anywhere else that I have seen, position and money talk words stronger than justice."

"And what of your position here, Nak?"

"It used to be that I was forever looking over my shoulders, but I've now learnt to divide myself from my previous incursions upon the British."

"Australia is but part of the British Empire. It grows all around us," added Abdul. "There's no escaping it."

"No escaping it and no joining it. We are here to earn our own living. This country needs us for the services we can provide, for without such services it would shrivel and die. They think they use us but it is we who have learnt to use them; and we must improve upon that learning as best we can."

Abdul felt an inner urge then to remind Nak of something that he had divulged in a letter to the importers of camels and their handlers prior to travelling to Australia, "I served with General Robert's Camel Transport Corps. I was in the march of 1880 from Kabul to Kandahar."

"I know," was all Nak said. He had arranged for word on Abdul's arrival, or someone similar, to fall in favour with his needs, so that he could receive a good working hand – he had many friends in Port Augusta. Abdul had arrived with the shipment of 1884 when 259 camels and thirty-five camel handlers were brought into the country. Nak had always preferred to feel the satisfaction of doing as he needed to do.

Recruiting Abdul was something he saw as fitting, avoiding the dregs that poured in and off of trains seeking employment. The demand for camel trade and services was high but work was hard to find, in particular now that more handlers were docked in Port Augusta and heading for Beltana.

"You served against the British and I served with them," Abdul continued.

"Why did you decide to answer my call for work?" asked Nak.

"It seemed the way to go; in particular where so many men and camels were bottle-necked into going no-place fast," answered Abdul, "and the man that grabbed my arm when I was lost and without work could talk fast and well. He persuaded me."

"Ah, yes... my old friend, Jehangir. He is a good man," and then Nak changed his tone. "Your escape from Afghanistan was no different than mine," said Nak. "We served those we needed to serve in order to find our place in life, but now... now we serve no one but ourselves. I sometimes regret my actions against my own when in Afghanistan but times were hard and I was pressed by my family's disposition, which I shan't talk about, to defend against the British and their incursions upon our country. But we must speak no more of this. War is a strange bedfellow. Besides anything else we are all Durranis and no different than Faiz Mahomet in a manner of speaking. Although he threatens our existence and job prospects we can still rely upon him if the need arises. You have no doubt heard that there is another in competition with him, Abdul Wade, a common and despicable Ghilzai. I'll spit upon his grave if I ever get the chance..." and Nak trailed off as he pondered the name of his new handler, for the Durranis were formerly known as the Abdulis.

"What of Shir?"

"He won't ask you of your dealings of war any more than he'll answer your questions about his dealings in it. For him the answer is as plain as the nose on your face."

"And that is?"

"That we have a new destiny and it is all the same to each of us, even though I am single, you are wed, and Shir is to be married."

"To be married?"

"Tonight," answered Nak, the grimace unchanging upon his face, the look in his eye reflecting the joy of the occasion, despite the bond between Shir and an Aboriginal being undesired.

"Is she an Afghan woman?"

"No," said Nak, "she is from here. She's an Aboriginal. A bride price has been paid and Shir will sleep little tonight. But tomorrow we must all be ready."

The concept of a bride price being paid was not formerly known by Aboriginals, but the failure in Afghan men to keep it disparate from their life in Australia had seen the Aboriginals take advantage. Afghan men had put into effect the idea of a 'bride price' being offered for their daughters very early on. No sooner had an Afghan man held in the power of his hand a daughter, whether she was from an Afghan woman or an Aboriginal, then he was requesting a bride price from any suitor able to pay: what goes around comes around.

"I assume that Shir is happy with the arrangements?"

"You will understand in time how lonely it gets here, so far away from home. You will be invited of course but currently we must provide you with the necessities of travelling with a camel string; getting you a blanket will do good to start for it can get very cold here by night, even in the hottest of summers; a good blanket is a comfort to sleep upon as well."

"Better than a woman," said Abdul as more of a statement than a question.

Nak laughed at the joke.

"Where are we going now?" asked Abdul.

"We'll go to where Shir is readying the supplies, counting and organising, confirming that we have enough camels ready for the task ahead."

"And if you don't have enough camels?" asked Abdul.

Nak turned to his new accomplice, "There are always enough camels in Hergott to purchase."

## CHAPTER FOUR

They weren't long in the hot pre-noon sun when they fell upon the suspecting Shir, his hand held tight to a checklist of necessities, each item being scrutinized as it was being placed into a pile a little distance from the opened gates of the shed in which the stores were being acquisitioned. Not only were there stores for the homestead in which they were required to ferry but also the day to day costs of living, where bags, sacks and tins of flour, sugar, rice, vegetables, oatmeal, potatoes, tea, baking powder and many, many other requirements were painstakingly ticked off from his long list.

This was where the true semblance of Marree's exemplary service fit into the scheme of the culture of the times, a divine replica of society from Australian towns from all around, Afghan and white being treated no different than another, for the colour of their money was all the same, but nothing, not a single grain of rice, would be paid for in advance; everything would be paid for when the task was complete and Shir had returned with money bags jingling and purses padded to high heaven in notes worthy of praise, or with a banknote glued to his hand.

"Ah, so this must be Abdul," said Shir as he prepared to shake hands with the new handler by shifting the tools of his current task into his left hand, much activity being conducted around them, men ferrying supplies here and there, conducting business as was the everyday occurrence.

"Yes," said Abdul with a smile, a most familiar look falling upon his eye indicating his train of thought, as all others had done when first meeting Shir, that yes, yes indeed, Shir was as ugly as sin and Abdul would be hard pressed to find someone as ugly; but he was a good man. "I'm pleased to find my way here into the company of two fine men."

"The work is hard," said Shir, "but we find it rewarding, as I'm sure you know already."

Abdul was unsure what to say in return for he had already been warned that talk of war was a 'strange bedfellow' and the last thing he wished to do was to commence his acceptance into their ranks with barbs of tension which might quite easily damage their friendship to come.

"My time as a cameleer was as varied as was the degree of tasks set upon, but from what I have seen of Australia I am sure to be in for an education."

"Desert here, desert there;" said Shir, "It's much the same wherever you go, only the camels change... as do the handlers," and looked to Nak.

"Shir is referring to the colonists," said Nak in a voice quietened by circumstance and knowing, even if he was speaking a different language and largely ignored by the white folk standing around. "They are stupid, one and all. There isn't a single man amongst the Europeans that can do nearly as good a job as us. We might live in the same town... separated as we are, maybe, but nevertheless, we command over the very essence of all which is to do with being a cameleer... and a good one at that."

Nak looked around and saw that Shir had attended to his responsibility with great affection as usual, "You've nearly finished, Shir."

"I wanted to get the job completed before this afternoon," answered Shir. "I have a wedding to attend to, or did you forget?"

"How can I forget," replied Nak as he looked to Abdul and

back again. "You've been reminding me every day for the past month." Nak looked again to Abdul. "Even in the middle of the desert, somewhere between here and Oodnadatta, all he can talk about is his wedding. I tell you this much, Shir; if I so much as hear a single whisper about your wedding after tonight I shall personally see to it that you sleep upon a nest of hornets, each and every night that we are gone from Marree."

"She will be sad to hear you say that," said Shir.

"Only if I say it in broken English," smiled Nak, referring to the point of fact that as an Aboriginal wife she understood nothing of Shir's language and extremely little of his place of birth.

"Nevertheless," defended Shir, "I shall promise right here and now that you'll hear nothing of my complaints nor bickering once we depart on the morrow: I promise."

"Don't make promises, Shir," said Nak. "You break your promises more often than you break wind."

Abdul burst out into a bout of laughter which caught many stares from all of those around, white, dark, black and brown, no matter what the colour of their skin they were all distracted by the laughter.

Abdul quickly took a grip of himself, "I'm sorry."

"Nothing to be sorry about," said Nak and looking at Abdul he added: "It's the beans that make him do it," and again Abdul burst out into laughter as his hands grabbed hold on his stomach to hold back the tearing pain of the joke.

"Come," said Shir, "help me finish with this lot, just a few minutes work remains and we can be off to prepare for tonight's sweet entertainment—."

"And the reception," cut in Nak.

"Ah, Nak," said Shir as he waved his finger in Nak's face. "You are tempting the good of our religion and faith by making such a remark. I would expect so much from a European, but not you, my friend."

"To have said nothing, would have been to allow a good opportunity to pass me by; besides, I am your friend."

"Come!" shouted Shir as he slapped Nak upon the shoulder, "you and Abdul help me finish and we can go home, to familiarize ourselves with one another prior to the wedding."

"Thank you, Shir," said Abdul.

"It's my pleasure," returned Shir with a slight bow.

## CHAPTER FIVE

The custom in Afghanistan was for a bride price to be paid to the family of the daughter who was to be wed, a custom that dated back to times that all had forgotten. A father could stand proud in knowing that he had received a good payment for his daughter, the most beautiful receiving the largest payment – which goes beyond saying. To a man the spoils of marriage were just that and where permission could be sought from a wife, and money allowed for the upkeep of more than one, a man could have as many wives as he could muster; there was no such thing as greed and nor was there any accusation of a man being cruel by doing so. It was quite normal for an old man in his fifties or sixties, let alone older than that, to pay for the affections of a young girl, a fourteen to eighteen year old girl of little experience in life being married off to an old man with a dirty mind full of lust, relishing the thoughts of grappling with such young flesh, running his rough and aged fingers up the inside leg of a girl that had barely reached puberty. So seldom did a young girl suffering in such a way let it be known; they simply suffered in silence.

Marriages were arranged between families for reasons of stability, money, position and greed: causes of manipulation to favour the father of the girl, to increase the effects of his life even if just slightly, a family's position amidst their society being increased marginally or more.

As it happened the circumstances in Australia were not much different. There was little 'bride price' administered in the earlier days when the Afghan's first arrived in Australia, but as men had daughters and these were bid for by other Afghan men, so the custom came into its effect and stabilised itself as the custom it always was.

Men were always on the lookout for women with stable figures, being slightly plump but not overly fat and it was this reflection of eagerness in the eyes of an Afghan which originally dissuaded Aboriginal women to accept the hand of a cameleer, even though they had little choice in the matter, for it was all up to the parent of the girl to either accept or decline any reasonable offer. Aboriginal women saw the look given by Afghan men towards those with the plumpest of figures, this being their prerequisite; as well as a proof behind what many had been told in open talk between family members: that Afghans ate human flesh and enjoyed it.

The Afghans themselves didn't know this and their only concern was for their status in life to be seen, if not heard, and a thin woman was a mark of poverty which lead to disrespect and sour looks; it was simply a sign of low status and a common handler of camels was lowly enough, unless such position was that of a jemadar, looking over and caring for many men and camels.

It was only with the life suffered together in the small town of Marree that an understanding between Aboriginal women and Afghan men commenced to grow, for both were as lonely as the other and Aboriginal life was breaking down as European ideas spread across the country both far and wide. There was little use of the word 'clan' and belief in tribal ways was decaying by the day. This was a time when Aboriginal women and Afghan men saw eye to eye and understood with a clearer picture the customs and way of life that the other maintained or held in the past. The white Australians treated both much the same and it was in this that both races fell into stride and developed a meagre interest in one-another.

It was quite unlawful at the time for a couple to live together in sin; marriage was the requirement, but where such a ceremony could not be afforded, for one reason or another, a relationship could be maintained in secret and with little knowledge of such liaison taking place; but this was not without its risks.

Women were not permitted to pray in the mosque of Marree and no other place was established for their divine right as the sexes were not permitted to pray together. Separate quarters were required and to this note the men were afforded closer spiritual comfort than the women. Inside the mosque there was a permanent feature which was present in all buildings of a similar nature, where location and materials allowed, and where not, a temporary replica or representation was placed: this was none other than the mirab which faced towards Mecca, and the Koran was laid to rest here until read, wrapped and resting upon a stool. By general standards the Koran was treated as a National flag for it wasn't permitted to be placed to rest beneath any other book. Shir's wedding was therefore undertaken with special customs taking place.

In order to pay homage to the general law of the country which most had accepted as their second home, or their primary, two marriage ceremonies were the act of all communions into this sacred ritual of devotion and harmony, even though most were wed out of sheer loneliness or forced into the relationship by a pressing father.

The order of the day was to have the marriage recognised by law and in this both Shir and his wife, Arika, had attended to register their joining just yesterday. It was now time to formally recognise their joining in accordance with Afghan law by undertaking the Islamic ceremony.

## CHAPTER SIX

Shir considered his wife and hoped she wasn't afraid. Her name in Aboriginal meant 'waterlily' and to him that was exactly what she was; his waterlily.

They were in separate rooms and prayers filled the air in Arabic, the ceremony led by the mullah of Marree, seeing to it that all custom was performed as required. Shir was dressed in nothing of particular flavour, ambition or excessiveness, nor was his wife; but he had a shalwar on – trousers that were wide at the top and narrow at the bottom, similar to pantaloons in appearance – and a turban of ivory-white, and Arika wore a dress of white with a veil, a cheap but acceptable offering to the ceremony.

Arika was comforted in her ordeal for she was lucky to have feelings for Shir as Shir had for her. Although she couldn't bestow unconditional love upon the man who was about to become her husband, she was able to commit herself to show that she felt the goodness of marriage fill her, the joy of heavenly bondage grip her loneliness and fill her with the joy of the occasion, she also had little choice but to accept Shir's religion and fulfil her daily life with the lifestyle and code of practise that every good Muslim followed. For anyone marrying an Afghan man the religion was not a by-product but a condition which simply had to be met and abided by, for there was no room, nor tolerance, for another religion.

The language, on the other hand, was something she would be fighting all her life but the words she shared with her husband would continue to be that of broken English, each knowing sufficient English to get them through the days.

There was also a huge feast to be attended, a celebration after the wedding to complete their transition from singles to a pair; she looked forward to that, to be showered with blessings and good fortune.

The dalak of Marree approached with a smile upon his face as though a line of boys had been prepared and made ready for their circumcision, each young man standing before him as eager as the other; but this was a wedding.

The dalak passed on his wishes with a bow and bestowed upon Shir a small amount of money which was his gift to him. The dalak was Zareen and he was a lowly man; not only was he the circumciser of boys but he was also the haircutter of the Ghantown. No one wished their daughter to be married to such a low caste man. The haircutter was in fact so lowly that there were only two others of less standing, and that was a thong and sieve maker, and a dancer.

"My best wishes to you and your new wife," said Zareen. "May Allah bestow upon you many favours."

"Thank you, Zareen," answered Shir, and although not having invited the man to the wedding ceremony as a main guest, he had insisted on his company for what the future might bring in the form of children and the fact that Zareen was a remarkable musician who played the flute well. It was uncanny how the feelings of despair and regret then hit Shir, for he felt that he had wronged the man that no one wished to seek when looking for a husband to take the hand of their daughter. Men looked for good payment for their daughters and lowly men had little, but Zareen... he had offered money to Shir, money which was scarce, and so Shir looked upon him differently that day.

Nak approached from the side as Zareen walked off with a smile, a facial expression that wouldn't be moved with a hundred lashes of a barbed wire stick. He stood beside him and his new wife and turned to look over the small gathering, tables full of food behind them, women in their veils and men in their turbans, all awaiting a continuance of the feast by pressing upon the tables and filling their plates.

"It is with great honour that I now ask you to make yourselves welcome here today by helping yourselves to this wonderful arrangement of refreshment," said Nak. "Shir thanks all of you for bringing what you have so that others may share in your wonderful presentations."

And without further ado the people moved slowly but surely with plates in hand to help themselves to all manner of food and drink, not a drop of alcohol in the house or an unkind word spoken on this day of great celebration.

Shir couldn't be happier as he looked upon his new bride, the Aboriginal woman who was remarkably beautiful for the life she had led. Living off the land in the desert, along the forages when creeks, rivers and streams flowed without restriction, under the scorching sun that beat down without remorse or the rain which beat down during the rainy season; none of its bleakness seemed to have been inherited by Arika, not a harsh days living showing upon her face. Most of all things that made Shir happy were the fact that she was also a plump little girl of just sixteen years of age, less than half his age; this alone was enough to make him very thankful and excited.

Arika was pleasantly comfortable in the surroundings of her new life and having spent a majority of it in Marree she was accustomed to the men and women of the Ghantown. Fear was present within her but at the moment it was at low tide and wouldn't surface until it was time to bring satisfaction to her husband. He hadn't pressed her for sexual favours during the time they had known one another and this she respected very much. The fact that Shir didn't force himself upon her offered feelings of security in thought that her father had made the right choice for her, and although Shir was an ugly man on the outside, he was a good man on the inside.

And this was the thought that remained with her when it was time to leave the feast room and all of those within it; the crowd dispersing after the ceremony had commenced to draw to a close. Shir's hand clenched hers for what was to come in this, their first night together.

Nak stood before the two with Abdul just to the rear of him, Abdul simply bowing with a smile, which was quickly returned.

"We're going to go now," said Nak. "I wish you both the very best, although your time together will be short, for tomorrow we depart and won't return for four weeks."

"Don't remind us," said Shir as he briefly looked upon his bride as she sat in silence to allow the men to speak. "Oh, I have several letters which I must give you, letters for the homestead when we arrive."

"Shir," said Nak with a lecture upon his voice. "You should not be thinking of work at this moment in time. I'll get the letters from you tomorrow when we load the camels."

"Very good," said Shir, and seemingly a little nervous opened his mouth to say something more. "What will you be doing tonight?"

"Nothing that should be concerning you, dear friend," answered Nak and departed without a further word.

Arika looked into her husband's eyes and spoke in English, her Afghan not ready to be attempted at such a time as this, "All nearly go home. We go too, soon. Is time for us."

"You are scared?"

"No," said Arika and then added something that she knew would excite her new husband, "wait no longer, look for good night with husband."

## CHAPTER SEVEN

Nak was now compelled, more than ever before in his entire life, to seek the comfort of one that he'd kept secret from the others, thoughts of Shir and his new wife getting the better of him.

He knew of a prostitute not too far away, she was a Japanese woman of average looks who often slept with Nak as he wasn't afraid to pay a little extra. He was a single man and the temptations of the soul were simply too much to bear, even for him. He deserved, as anyone else, to feel the gratifying warmth of female flesh upon the palm of his hands, to be stroked and fondled as his desires screamed out in mounting frustration.

Why was it so easy to give in to the lures which manifested from within his manhood? It wasn't for Nak to answer, but simply to see the urge satisfied, the frustration quenched, for it was going to be a long time before he'd have the opportunity again.

She lived in a part of the Ghantown which was away from the remainder for she was considered unclean by many and never given the opportunity to make friends with those of respectable disposition, but what might be respectable in Marree was considered a dilapidated eyesore to those of the big city, and so she remained aloof of the Afghan Ghantown, the services she provided only tolerated in order to restrain the single man's anxieties.

Her real name was unknown by the community at large but not to the men that pressed visit upon her. She was known as Saki to most men but given pet names by some, and although she was shunned and kept at bay, neither recognized or provided the comforts of a community at large, she led a reasonably pleasant life, even though lonely for the most part. Her life was full of unpleasantness but criticism was largely ignored; those that paid and displayed the most discourtesy upon her were those that were new to the Ghantown.

Nak thought heavily upon the ambitions of Saki and understood, quite clearly, how misfortune played its part within the scheme of her chosen profession. She'd been married off to a much elderly man, a Chinese businessman whose interests in her quickly collapsed just weeks before his death, for he also had strong feelings for his cook. He had been a rough and bad man, kind to those that knew him best, but always slapping and punching his wife behind closed doors. For her there was nothing left in life but to make the best of what it had to offer, and to sleep with men for a wage was better than sleeping with an old man for little more than eyeful of fist. Left alone in a world she didn't understand, and without any real prospect of finding a husband, anyone to look after her, or a decent job to be made advantage of, she'd left Adelaide behind her to escape the racketeers.

Stuck in the outback with no money, except a few coins that might have been otherwise owed to the unscrupulous wielders of bad fortune, she soon found herself serving men the only way she knew how. And Nak thought about the opportunities that might be offered to him in the future, where a wife could be sourced from the Ghantown at any time in the years to come; but where would such a wife come from, in particular when considering his grimacing facial expression. Saki had more to offer Nak than even she knew.

Money; that's what was needed, and he'd quickly set himself up an account where savings could be hoarded away from prying eyes, for a future that would see him be the same as others he knew; a married man with children. Saki had come to mind; she always came to mind.

Unfortunately, it was entirely impossible for any of the Asian women to be married to an Afghan; it was simply unheard of. All Asian women refused to look upon the Afghan men as a possible husband-to-be, and as for most prostitutes of the time, Saki maintained little decorum and she disgusted all of those trying to better their lives, all around trying to live in harmony with everyone else, a life lead by religion and without fault, the characteristics of a well-manicured town being the esteemed ambition of most in a society fighting off prejudice by living together in such a confined space.

Prejudice was always present but in the outback towns it seemed to be tolerated more than elsewhere, for everyone's existence did depend upon cooperation, and cooperation was something Saki lived without.

Nak finally fell upon the out-of-the-way shack, a dry creek bed of little worth just behind and in good location to carry away great masses of water, and very quickly, at times that the weather turned bad – or fruitful depending on your frame of thought. There were a few date palms growing nearby that seemed to be thriving and the window shutters of the small building were closed with a single item of clothing hanging from a clothesline, a flag of familiarity which meant that Saki was home and ready to please.

Nak approached the shack and as he passed the clothesline he pulled the worn shirt from its position and placed it upon a barrel next to the front door. He knocked twice and waited: he didn't wait long.

Saki opened the door and smiled as the light of the moon cast itself upon her face, the shadow of the door moving across her, folds of her body disrupting the lay of the shadow upon her form, the outline of her breasts seen for what they were and her hips and slight plumpness coming to view.

She was a delight to look at, more beautiful to Nak than anyone else he'd ever laid eyes upon – which was easy to interpret from the point of view that very few women looked upon Nak with any respect or interest.

Respect: two issues; a single action. The action was sexual but the issues were of separate embodiments. Saki was looking for coins to pass her palm and Nak was after a night of lust.

"Good night," said Nak with a smile in the best English he could muster, for Saki knew less of Nak's language than she knew of the women who lived a little way down the dirt track and towards the main hub of life and activity in Marree.

"Yes," said Saki in reply. "Please, enter," and she opened the door and stood aside so that Nak could continue his night of excitement, entering the shack which was lit by a single lantern, several silks hanging from the walls, a rug of thick wool and a bed pushed aside in the corner, large and comfortable, Saki's place of work and confinement; there was little else in the shack other than a bench top and several wash basins – she did her cooking out of doors beneath an adjoining shelter.

"I go work, long time," said Nak.

Saki simply smiled at the information, the grimace upon Nak's face quite hideous, but Saki was used to such ugliness in her business and ignored what she saw with great compassion, great skill, and with much ease.

She moved over to where he stood, near the edge of the bed that he had come to play upon.

"I stay long time," said Nak as he pulled the colour of money from his pocket. Saki continued to smile and moved her hands skilfully over his body, feeling every slender curve offered by Nak's thin build.

Nak then returned the gestures of a formality he had come to know and enjoy, lifting his right hand to her breast and placing his left in behind the small of her back. He tenderly kissed her with much effort, the pain upon his lips evident with the strain. Saki took control then and did the kissing for them, rolling her lips and tongue over the coarse tissue of Nak's mouth and then removed herself from his mild embrace, taking several steps back from him. She pulled lightly upon the restraints of her thin gown and let it slip from her body, her nipples coming to full view and Nak's manhood became fully aware of its function in this ritual of his.

The stresses of his life were about to be lifted, he would soon be able to concentrate more healthily on the task before him, and without further ado they stepped towards one another and embraced.

## CHAPTER EIGHT

The following morning was presented the usual ceremony of prayer and singing from the Muslims in the Ghantown as was customary and expected, the sounds of the mystic verses reaching the far voids of what was known as Marree and a town on the edge of civilization, though one would be hard-pressed to say it was on the edge of despair.

Shir had said good farewell to his plump wife by having his way with her for the fifth time in a single night and had seen to it that Abdul was provided good companionship by meeting him at his shack of residence, a single room building of corrugated iron that had been offered to him for the comfort of rest, shared with five others – the family of Goulam Bauz who was currently on a job to Oodnadatta.

"Good morning to you, Abdul," greeted Shir as he advanced on the new companion as he stood in front of the shack with a small bag of essentials in his hand, "for a good morning it is. I hope your night was comfortable."

"It was," answered Abdul. "Thank you for finding such good company for me. The home of Bauz was most obliging and friendly."

"As all are, here in Marree," said Shir as he closed the gap and Abdul fell in beside him for the walk to where the camels would be waiting. "You would be too put out to be asked to find anyone of sour nature. The community here would be no different than what you were used to back in your village in Afghanistan."

"I would say, in all matter of fact, that the company was

better," said Abdul with a smile, falling into stride with his new friend as they walked towards several corrals, lines placed between posts where camels were tied and waited for their turn to be loaded and placed within a string.

Nak could be seen beside the enclosure as he waved to gain their attention and before they knew it they were together once more.

"You look refreshed," said Nak of Shir.

"Refreshed and tired," he answered. "You too, look... happy."

"I sought the company of an old friend last night," replied Nak, and although he never mentioned Saki by name, most of those that knew Nak the best understood his relationship with the prostitute that 'lived-down-the-road'.

"Then we are all in good fortune," added Abdul, unaware of Nak and his night of lust, "for I too had good company in the form of a small family."

"Yes," acknowledged Nak. "We have shared many favours, us two and Goulam. It would be hard to find a better man than he."

Abdul looked over towards the camels attached to the line between posts and asked, "Are those our camels?"

"Yes," answered Nak. "I tied them up early this morning so that they would be more easily and quickly taken to where the stores will be laid."

Abdul nodded, seeing for himself that many other camels stood unrestrained in the corral, awaiting their masters and a hard day's work.

Shir then handed Nak, the jemadar, two letters for the homestead in which they were to lay visit with supplies. It would be the last letters delivered by hand as a mail service had just been put into effect and commenced by Jack Hester, a service that would only grow as the demand for news and information flowed thick and strong between settlements and towns in the outback; the cameleers could only hope that the need for strong resilience in the form of camel strings didn't go the same way and fall to the whims of game-changers, bullocks or horses.

"I was handed this by the Postmaster late yesterday," said Shir.

Abdul was impressed and said, "It's good that word spreads and that people know one another here."

"The Europeans... or colonists: they are all the same... they have their differences of opinion and there is some division between us all," said Shir, "but they see fit to ensure that service is provided to those that reside in the settlements around, no matter how small or large. But believe me, if it was to a settlement owned by Muslims, there would be a different sense of urgency upon the Postmaster's willingness to provide assistance."

"But we will deliver the letters, regardless," added Nak. "Who knows, it could be for an order of more wool than we are expected to pick up, hence a larger reward in terms of wage when the task is complete."

"You never know," said Shir. He looked to Abdul, "There is always that, as Nak has advised. But let's talk on this more at a later time; we have camels to move and supplies to attend."

"Good," said Abdul. "I shan't forget this day; my first real work in this country."

"And it won't be your last," said Shir, "for there will be work where we continue to provide a great service, and we must work harder than anyone else in order to retain good customer satisfaction."

"When we do well for a settlement or homestead, we always receive further work," finished Nak, proud of his accomplishments as drawn from his stance as he pulled back his shoulders and shifted his head.

Abdul was rather proud to have a job, and with good people to accompany him on the long treks across Australia.

## CHAPTER NINE

Abdul was in Australia, as all before him, on a three year contract, but where records fail the administration the imported will take advantage, and the news was soon provided to him, that he would end up staying till his heart was content or the hunger to return to Afghanistan got the better of him.

Abdul could only ponder the future which was yet to be cast for him, at this very minute in time, although inexperienced as he was with familiarity in regards to Australia, he considered one thing and one thing only. The comparison between the two countries, the hardships dealt to him day after day; all of it seemed to be one and the same. So what was it for him to hunger for Afghanistan?

He was a free man with no ties apart from the fact that he was married with two children, but others had abandoned their responsibility, so why not he? He wouldn't be the first to remain in Australia with family in Afghanistan. It was then that the pain of the thought hit his heart like a stab in the gut by a recently sharpened knife, long and broad, a cutting edge of teeth set to tear him apart from the inside out. He couldn't abandon his family, would never leave them to their own vices. If life in Australia could not afford him the option of importing his family so that they could stand by his side in this new life, no matter how long that life may be, then he would go back to them, dead or alive, on two feet or wrapped up in a blanket or cloth. Whatever the cost, Abdul considered his only alternative; to work his finger's to the bone and never complain, nor shirk a job. There was very little to him that meant more than his family. In some ways he felt as though he had deserted them but in reality he was doing what he knew was in the best interest for them all. The cards had been dealt him and now he needed to play the game.

The camel string was relatively easy to get moving, tying each by a long rope, neck to neck, an informality which wasn't the normal condition for handling camels prior to loading with stores and connecting nose pegs, but Nak was anxious to on the way, for it was a four week return trip to the homestead and back, taking the drastically close to the onset of a possible downpour of the likes none of them wished to experience more than they had to. Rain could be as treacherous as a sandstorm and the one thing Nak wished to avoid was any unnecessary delay, for the current consignment of wool from the homestead was required in Marree with such time restraints that the threesome would barely have time enough to scratch themselves more than once a day.

The initial process, as for the most part of what was to be carried out on the caravan, was nothing superiorly different or more difficult than what Abdul had known or experienced in the past, but routine played a big part in the process of preparing a string for the road as much as setting the camels down for the night after a long day's work.

## CHAPTER TEN

The camels were tied in order of advance, from lead camel to the kitchen, the order of march in which the camels would find themselves once commenced upon their journey towards Birdsville, an order that they all knew and had come to be comfortable with. One of the camels came under the scrutiny of Abdul.

"You have a pregnant camel," he voiced.

"Yes," said Nak, none too concerned over the situation. "She'll give birth in a few days."

"It's not my place, but wouldn't she be better left behind?" asked Abdul.

"The camels are used to hard work, whether pregnant or not," answered Nak. "Besides, we can't afford to leave her behind and secondly the remainder of the string would miss her. Every camel here has its place. It's too upsetting to have one missing from its place in the line."

Little further was spoken other than a few words of affection and urging from the cameleers to their camels, Abdul commencing his introduction to the many names that flowed from Nak's and Shir's mouths. Each and every camel had a name and each was known at a glance. They were different sizes and of course, different colours. Dull greyish brown or yellowish brown where the hair grew the longest, and at shoulders and hump the colour changed in most concerns to brown. The hair at the mane also grew brown but the main coat was a slate grey, shades of black, chocolate, cream, and several of those in the caravan were white, a rare colour indeed. All had their characteristics, each was known for its abilities, likes and dislikes; they were family to both Shir and Nak.

Abdul was wondering about the situation with the saddles for the camels when the supplies came into view. He saw two Aboriginal boys hard at work setting saddles down into three lines, the centre line of saddles facing the opposite way to the other two. They were tidying up their task when the camels were led in and the string cut into three parts.

The twenty-four camels were now eight to a line and lead into position under guidance by the cameleers into their 'line of advance', the front and rear-most rank facing one direction and the centre most facing the opposite, Abdul following Nak's advice and the urging of one of the Aboriginal boys, whose teeth sparkled white through the darkened lips upon his face. The camels were soon positioned, each placed in front of the pack saddle which rested in place upon the dry ground.

"What are their names?" asked Abdul.

"That one there, closest to you; he's Amaroo," said Nak and as the name was mentioned he looked over and smiled briefly, "the other is Girra: it's the name given to a creek or a tree, but I don't know which."

"Amaroo is 'a beautiful place', a strange name for a boy," added Shir.

"They work hard and for very little," said Nak. "It's to their abilities that they serve us well by remembering how to lay the saddles down, each camel knowing his by smell."

"I've never seen a camel accept another's in good stead," said Shir as he commanded the camels under his control to sit, each lined up with his saddle. "Just there... that's it, Abdul." Some of the camels proceeded to sit without a word. "Some know their place well; it's only the lazy ones that need a whisper in the ear or a hit with a stick."

"A sting in the leg brings back memory rather fast," said Nak as his camels sat in place.

Abdul looked down the line to the eight under his control.

"Mine must be lazy, there are still six standing," observed Abdul.

"No, Abdul," said Shir. "They're testing you; that's all. Show them who's boss and they'll quickly learn."

With all twenty-four camels sitting in position the saddles were placed upon them with expert hands, the cameleers working marvellously fast, faster than any white man could do. One man stands to either side of a camel and quite purposely ensures that the pack saddle is secure before placing the load simultaneously, it being balanced upon the pack saddle with remarkable expertise.

Saddles were built with different interests in mind; firstly the packing of supplies upon a camel's back, and secondly, the comfort of the rider should a seat upon the animal be preferred to walking: or weight restraints permitted a rider to mount alongside the supplies.

A riding saddle was a simple creation of two forks, one in front and one behind the camels' hump. These were connected by a horizontal bar with an extension to the rear, the rider sitting upon a leather-covered seat with feet in stirrups. It was to many colonists' surprise to see that few Afghans allowed themselves the comfort of such a price position of being so high from the ground, most preferring to take their positions beside their strings where the control was more easily displaced and each was ready to react to any emergency that might unfold in their day's journey; and leather pouches and bags could easily be attached or simply flung over the camel's back.

Removing the pack saddles by night was one of many of the cameleers' duties, and painstakingly checking each individual camel was something that simply had to be performed before and after a day's labour. The loss of a single camel would have been too much to bear in regards to the cost in replacing it and the ability to continue with the load they had in transit – even though it was quite easy to shift the loads around between camels – was simply another task that required time, and time was more important to them than their own stomachs which would tremble with hunger during the long hours of daylight.

Pack saddles might need to be relined with jute, strong fibre from wool bales or wheat sacks, and in this, Nak preferred straw. It didn't occur too often but on occasion an un-muzzled camel of poor temperamental disposition might try drawing the stuffing on the saddle or stores before him, snatching what he could from the camel in line, not to mention bite at the rear-end of the camel in the string to his front. Where possible, Nak preferred to keep his animals free from bondage but always carried several muzzles for such an emergency.

The straw of the saddles was placed in through small slits and forced home by a wooden driver and mallet. With time the straw would turn to chaff due to movement and need to be replaced, a never-ending cycle of replenishment due to the creation of a bulge which created sores upon the camels' back. And here came the question of doubt which lingered on many minds; the option of travelling by night. Night offered a cooler trip and freed the cameleers of their duty to perform their prayers, but travelling by day was better in the long run as a good meal could be taken in by the Afghans at last light, in particular during times of fasting, and the camels allowed to feed once placed on short hobbles.

Saddle sores were to be avoided at all costs; the last thing needed was for a camel to become infested with a back sore that turned septic by becoming a fly-blown lesion that caused death. But their feet were also checked on a daily basis, ensuring that each was free from cuts and abrasions.

Yes indeed, Shir and Nak loved their camels as though they were family.

The loading of the camels came next, an arduous task to say the least. Much attention to detail was placed upon the loading, not only for the benefit of the camels but also the work to be endured during the last part of the day when the load was to be removed from the camels for the night.

Thongs and cordage were tied in such a way that they could be more easily removed in such quick fashion that the time was taken each morning to ensure that supplies were secured correctly.

The men's knees did most of the lifting but backs too were strained where straining should be avoided.

Loading was carried out prior to nose pegs being attached so that the animals could be more easily attended to with their loads starting from behind them and simply picked up, carried forward, and then tied into position. Nose pegs were then placed on.

The ability for a camel to be subjected to a bit in the mouth was non-existent and in respect to this the only other real alternative was for a nose peg of hardwood to be inserted. The sensitivity of the camels at the nose was such that a rude awakening would be jolted through each, via the use of the nose peg, when acting disruptively. Nose pegs permitted much easier control over the animal in strings than without and to pursue control by any other means was simply out of the question.

The nose peg was more cone-shaped than not and never made of heat-conducting metal, and was attached to a length of cordage long enough to be connected to the tail of the camel to its front with a sag between in order to reduce the strains upon the cordage during movement... such was life when a frightened camel jerked its head around, breaking the connection of the nose peg; but cameleers always sought to offer a reasonably pain-free existence, even if it meant that extra work was to be suffered, for they were seen on the odd occasion putting slow chase to a concerned camel with broken line prior to placing it back in file with the others of the string.

Of all the days before them this was the most time-consuming, for loading in the days to come would see to it that the camels would be in a more favourable position, one man required to stand either side of a camel with the load to be deposited upon the camel's back and secured into position with leather thongs and cordage.

The men worked their way down the three lines, fondling the camels affectionately as they preceded, Nak kissing the camels delicately, showing that he cared for them more than he cared for anyone else in the world... and then Saki came into mind, his exploits from the night before where he felt as though he were in heaven.

The last camel in line, which followed the other of his species so well, with little interest in mind, was the kitchen camel. He was much like the others, to simply step along in line, little to look forward to but the dreary hours of looking at nothing but the rear-end of the camel to his front.

The kitchen camel was so named as it was the camel with the mobile kitchen with gallons of water carried for 'specific needs'. It was upon the saddle, upon the hide, that this creature heard the consistent banging and clanging of any loose equipment, for his duty was to carry all manner of pot and pans, utensils for cooking and eating, food, camp oven and several tarpaulins which could quite easily be erected to hold back a miserable night of strong wind or heavy rain. But some fortune does shine down upon the seemingly least favoured for his load would diminish in weight whereas the others would have to continue each day with the knowledge that what was endured one day would be endured the next, and also that for no particular reason, he was the last to be loaded.

The three men attended their camels as expertly, if not more-so, than a soldier practising his drill movements on a drill square before heading off to war.

Abdul looked the lead camel in the face, the camel familiar with Nak more than he, for Nak was the jemadar and the camel knew it. His hare lip seemed more prominent than any of the others in the string, and Abdul grinned at a thought that crossed his mind. It was the story of Muhammad and how he kissed a camel upon the lips for escorting him through an enemy camp unheard; the upper lip parted, and a gift was bestowed upon it and all his descendants: from this day forth all camels would not only have hare lips but would move silently wherever it should wonder.

In a little under forty minutes the camels were all ready to go, loaded with all the requirements of the caravan and the needs of the homestead. Only one other addition was required and this was the weapon that Nak carried with him.

Nak looked up and down the rifle that he cradled in his hands. Al Halal meat was a part of everyday life here in Marree, for the Afghans and their religion, and for those that provided it. Although such meat was to be properly prepared for killing it wasn't unheard of for cameleers to carry out the preparations themselves when far from home and without a source of meat in which to sustain them during the long and hard hours of travelling to and from settlements. The hardest part of the transition from beast of burden to jerked meat was the actual jerking itself, for it was time consuming and took from the cameleer's valuable hours, a very good reason for a good supply of meat to be carried in the first place.

In most cases, in particular the smaller Ghantowns, it was the task of the butcher – who was also the mullah – to see to it that all animals were killed al Halal; all was carried out to the strict guidelines of the Koran. All meat was thus purified by the swift movement of a knife across the jugular whilst fully conscious and the mullah faced towards Mecca.

Animals killed in this way were left to bleed, the blood draining from the body and carrying with it any germs that might otherwise create any amount of intimidation and putrefy. With one's state of mind put at ease came the answer to a hungry belly.

The long strips of salted meat that Nak had made available to the three of them, meat of a goat which had been awaiting slaughter and drying, would be enough to supply them with protein until such a time that it ran out, it was therefore quite necessary for Nak to take along with him a rifle in which to kill a wild bullock or kangaroo. In this the hardest part of the task was not actually shooting the animal but to actually run up to it and slit its throat before the animal in question died, at the same time voicing the following prayer towards Mecca, 'Bismillah Wallahu Akbar', meaning that the sacrifice had been made to Allah and that permission was hence sought for the animal to be used for human consumption... if the animal died before this could be carried out then the animal was left to rot.

To this note and nagging thought Nak fondled the trigger and sights of the weapon he carried, ensuring all was clean, before placing it into its bag for possible use at a later date, fully loaded and ready to fire.

The packing and loading was now complete and with the lifting and strapping finished the two Aboriginal boys scarpered off to see what mischief they could find, their palms carrying a little money, their wage for the time spent helping the cameleers, help which was altogether needed but provided more for better relations between the two people, being both a different colour and of different religious belief as compared to those from other parts of the world or born unto Australia: they were unique.

Nak took his position at the head of the caravan, leading the string with little effort, for the lead camel knew his part in the scheme of things, leading the others into the wilderness which was to be their home for some time to come.

It wasn't long before the last of the Ghantown shacks fell behind them and the noises offered by the desert embossed themselves quite heavily upon the three men; the solace of the next two weeks only broken by them and them alone: and the twenty-four camels which they attended.

## CHAPTER ELEVEN

The camels in their string were all from India, or of descendants that came from there. They were hard and fast, not a lazy bone amongst them, though some did bare reflection of that uncommon label. The heat of the Australian outback meant little to them, shrugged off like an annoying fly, over 104 degrees [40 degrees Celsius] on most days, and that was in the shade of the coolest tree, the weather being hottest in the early part of the afternoon.

There was no escaping it, no relief in sight, and all the string could do was to follow the lead camel who in all his glory held his head up high with his master to his right, the cameleer so familiar leading the way to their destiny where wages could be secured for the work that they performed.

The camel was so much better than a horse, in all respects and in particular in regards to height. Travelling through Spinifex country was not bad for a camel for he was so tall and carried his load out of reach of most of the lower branches of scrub where damage could be done to bags of all description.

A tell-tale sign of many hours' march through such terrain was the marks left by a caravan, the first three feet of a camel's leg being shred bare of all hair, the lower portions as black as night and as shiny as a new pair of boots. But their skin was as hard as nails and no harm came to them, whereas with a horse the skin would be torn to pieces. But without the Spinifex the Australian outback would be little less than another desert of the African north or savanna. The plant helped prevent erosion and provided a retreat for birds and other wildlife, not to mention that the Aboriginals used the plant as a resource by using it to the best of their abilities, to secure spear points to shaft and stone-sharpening tools to a woomera handle.

This was saltbush country edged with mulga where the sandhills undulated across the land for as far as the eye could see and the rabbit burrows that infested the ground were beyond belief.

Rabbit provided something different to eat, the white meat providing great satisfaction, so long as it was killed in the customary fashion as required of a Muslim; which wasn't easy to procure as a single shot from the rifle usually meant the immediate death of the animal. There were also plenty of emu and kangaroo, but so seldom was one caught and eaten.

The mulga was a good meal for the camels but such animals can't live on mulga alone. The camel didn't carry water internally such as in reservoirs, although it did have the ability to reabsorb its own urine to a degree, but it was very efficient at extracting moisture from plant life such as mulga and paracelia. The hump, in contradiction to many voiced opinions, was in fact its fat storage and a camel which was fed poorly had a reduced hump when compared to those that maintained a healthy disposition. There were other aspects of the camels' disposition that came into play on the desert lands. Their pads were soft and enabled them to move much more easily across sand, to take short cuts between different parts of the worn track trodden hard by a million hoofs; their soles are hardy and take heat, cloven-hoofed and seemingly made for hard labour.

They had an uncanny sense of direction and memory, and would know where they were going if they had been there before. They could travel three miles an hour, eight to ten hours a day, with the cameleers singing traditional songs as they walked beside them, neither stopping for rest during the day nor for anything to eat, for lunch was too labour intensive and camels couldn't stand in one spot with a load upon their backs for very long.

The camels had great observation and they tended to look around all the time and if they saw something strange or out of place then they would stare at it for a long time as they walked towards and past the object of curiosity, and next time they came past this same place they would look in that direction expecting to see it again, no matter what it was, be it a dingo or other animal that has scared it in the past, or simply a small tent, torn clothing hanging from a limb, or bush or tree that stood out amongst the surrounds.

They were a most remarkable animal.

## CHAPTER TWELVE

As they continued on into the wilderness the hours dropped off behind them, the sun peaking at noon, but not the built up of heat that still had room for further gains as the day wore on into the afternoon on this, their first day.

The figure of someone could be seen up ahead and the eyes of the lead camel fell on the object of his curiosity, a dark-brown to almost black camel of many years experience and named Chocolate for obvious reasons. It was a known fact that Nak had an almost pure black bull and that for more than anything else that the remainder of all of the camels within his string were yellowish brown and had dark manes; but certainly not all.

Nak loved this beast almost more than life itself, a working pet that was a companion on long treks across open plains of undulating nothingness. He looked up into the camel's eyes and saw that his attention was most assertively retained upon the dark mass that drew closer and closer as the caravan closed the gap upon the seated form of a man.

They came upon the Aboriginal who looked worse for wear and on passing him saw that he was a victim of his mother's cruelty, the three Afghans unable to refrain from looking upon his miserable state, the condition of his life forever affected by such horrendous actions against him that he would be forever shunned by those that came into close contact with him.

They'd heard of this man, both Shir and Nak, even though to Abdul he was nothing more than a sorrowful sack of flesh, seated their upon the side of the road with his palm held out flat, hoping it to be filled with food, the Aboriginal man being a shell of emptiness and emotionally scarred for life. But food he would not receive for the cameleers had only enough for themselves, and barely that, and if their journey was to falter by the way and be increased by so much as a day then they would find themselves without food, too.

His name had been forgotten but he was known as a wanderer, a man bound to the land for ever and a day, to walk the stretches of track and desert until his dying day. It seemed at first sight that he was smiling and happy to see someone... anyone of the real world; yet the reason he was seen to bare his teeth to the world was due to other matters which turned the eyes of many Europeans.

His mother had burnt his lips away when he was very young, a mother tired of his constant crying for food, and where a mother is bound by the viciousness of alcohol she always bears the brunt of its evil. What sort of mother would do such a thing to a loving child, a little one that clung to the one that had delivered him to the world?

A young child knows nothing of formality or the ways of the world until taught or experienced. How could a mother, no matter how deranged, lose all manner of semblance and pick up a red hot stick from the burning furnace of a fire and burn away the lips of the one she was supposed to care for?

But that was the way it was and as the string continued on its way the men could only look on with sadness and continue with the task at hand, and not so far up the track, out of sight of the one to their rear, another Aboriginal came into view. It was a half-caste, a person to be tormented all their life.

Pasted over the land, like freckles upon a face, was the 'yeller-feller', an encumbrance to society. Neither wanted by the Aboriginal community, nor the white folks alike, these half-castes were treated as nothing more than pests by all except their mother. Was it no wonder then that the strength in number of women begging for food began to be an encroachment upon all those that fell upon them during their task to supply farms and portage their merchandise back to a station where they could continue on to market.

These Aboriginal women were constantly selling themselves short, accepting a little coin or food so that a white man could partake of a little pleasure, to have his way with a woman, regardless of creed, nationality, colour of her skin, or standing in life, and then to throw her aside. Many men had been caught short by a woman showing up at his side with a baby in her arms, but none would shoulder the responsibility.

So it was that this old woman with a baby, abandoned to the world, to her own devices, caught the glances of Chocolate and the three men as per the previous Aboriginal they had recently passed. It was a shrewd awakening to Abdul, a presentation of a new world, the introduction to an Australia that wasn't advertised back at home before he'd decided to take the plunge and travel far from his family.

Abdul was here to make his fortune, to send money back to his family at home, and the real awakening of his future was now, more than ever, shrouded in doubt. He had seen very little in this land of fortune which was to appease him, make him rich, or do him the justice he believed he deserved. He had served in the army for the British Empire... wasn't Australia just that, an extension of that which he had served? He was owed more than this.

And as they continued on, none breaking their stride, several pots and pans came loose and clanged a metallic melody as the kitchen passed the mother and her baby, teasing her with what she would not receive.

## CHAPTER THIRTEEN

The day continued rather quickly after the two scenes of Aboriginal neglect, the minds of the three men filled with questions and few answers, but Abdul's was in full swing, contemplating hard all that he had seen as the sun commenced to approach the edge of civilization, and a beautiful red and orange sky filled the horizon for as far as the eye could see.

In the midst of summer, as it was upon the land in which the camels had come to know as their second home, a place in which to make a fortune, it was as hot as the deserts of any other place on Earth, where camels were quickly trained to go without water for up to two weeks, three being possible, and when the opportunity arose to drink from a bucket, up to 20 gallons would be taken in, fuel that was the requirement for any creature that walked on two legs or four, or even wriggled upon the ground as a serpent does so well. So, to compare Australia with other desert regions of the world was realistically permitted.

The creek beds around were dry and cracking, bush, trees, and grasses yellow like straw and almost devoid of all nourishment, and apart from the morsels that could be extracted by a hungry camel, the string forever keeping an eye open for good opportunity, for they would be in hobbles soon enough and could make their way back to any place within reasonable distance, to eat at their pleasure and to have their fill.

It was best to place short hobbles upon the camels by night as opposed to the long hobble as this restriction within the camels' ability to move ensured that it didn't wander off too far by night, for the last thing the cameleers wished was to be displaced for hours on end searching for lost camels in the bush when time restraints were upon them and the sun was reaching over the horizon to get its first glimpse of the land before it. In this the two front legs were restrained and the camels never wandered more than a mile or two from the campsite, and when they did it was always together with the lead camel maintaining status over the others, and where one goes the others are sure to follow.

The men were always on the lookout for saltbush, spinifex and mulga during an advance from point of departure to destination, for the camel had a mind that put other animals to shame, its memory being of remarkable calibre. It was to this habitual practise of camels wandering off into the desert in search for food that each wore a brass bell around its neck attached to a bright coloured ribbon that might more readily stand out in the bleak contrast of the sandy dunes around, for it was very hard to see a camel over any great distance when the country was literally littered with spinifex, saltbush and mulga. For this reason above all others, Chocolate was an advantage, for he stood out more than the others and was usually first seen when sought.

## CHAPTER FOURTEEN

And so to unloading, the threesome began their work, at a place where a little comfort could be received, the last remnants of drawn out shade disappearing into the night as darkness fell quite rapidly upon them.

There wasn't any great concern for the men to hurry, for the light of the moon would soon offer itself freely and the stars above the clear night sky would provide additional illumination.

The camels were brought in alongside the campsite and ordered to kneel, loads still upon them. Their forelegs folded beneath them and then front legs onto knees, back legs folded and then down onto hindquarters, and the loads were prepared for removal by Shir and Nak, starting from Chocolate and progressing to the rear as they loosened the thongs and cordage. As this was done, Abdul untied the nose peg from the camel being attended, to the camel to its rear, so that a loaded pack – where applicable – on the camel's back could be lifted by the men either side and then placed to the rear, front, or side. In this the cameleers were rehearsed well but each string had a different jemadar and each jemadar his mind set at a particular practise. It was most useful to place the loads, where light enough to be lifted, to the front of the camel that was carrying it, in this way the camel would seat itself before the load when loading was to take place early each morning, for each camel knew the smell of its own pack. In fact, Nak and Shir had a different practise for each caravan they attended.

For the most part it was a simple operation. With thongs and cordage pulled loose the loads were allowed to fall both left and right of the camel in question, the saddles then removed and placed at the head. Each load was secured to form a compact bundle of supplies which were easily manipulated, positioned and tied. As each saddle was placed before the camel the camel was allowed to stand, a hobble quickly placed upon its feet before being allowed to search for food; it wasn't possible to secure hobbles whilst a camel was seated on all fours.

The cameleers worked with remarkable speed, the essence of the task rehearsed in their heads prior to bringing the camel train to a halt, and after their work was done there was praying to be carried out and of course the meal which was to be eaten in the comparative darkness, for the sun was down and the moon was yet to show itself in its fullest splendour that it had to offer, but steadily it climbed its way into the heavens above.

## CHAPTER FIFTEEN

Their camp was rudely prepared, prayer mats placed upon the ground beside one another and sticks for a campfire quickly prepared as the camels went about their task of finding food to eat, never straying too far from the lead camel, Chocolate. Tents were not prepared this night as the wind was low and no rain was expected, but sleeping blankets were drawn from the supply horse in front of the kitchen camel's load and laid upon the ground still rolled up tight to deter any likely intrusion of unwanted pests or reptiles.

It was a common misconception that Muslims should face the east when performing their daily prayers but there was a small point of fact that didn't elude Nak and Shir, who were quick to point out their knowledge to Abdul. Mecca was closest to Australia via the north-west and so this is the direction in which all prayers were cast.

Being on the road between homesteads and settlements was no excuse to refrain from prayer for the headman or jemadar of every group would carry a copy of the Koran and read from it as required at the times of the day identified as sacred to them all.

Their religion was everything to them and for the cameleers their faith was the 'five pillars of Islam'. Prayer was a crucial part of their daily life and separated them from the colonists, binding Muslims together as one, and where they should be in the middle of nowhere, be it alone or with others tied to the restraints of a string of camels, time would be taken to spread their prayer mats upon the ground, face towards Mecca, and conduct ablutions as laid down within their book of high esteem. As for the five pillars there were also five periods in the day in which prayer was to take place.

Ablutions were also an unnecessary waste of water and easily drew a barrage of discontent from the eye sockets of Christians and other men. It was custom for the water to be running and free of disease, to be clean of insects and larvae, the body parts to be washed prior to prayer being the face, hands, forearms and feet. But here in the desert where water was scarce another alternative was formed and so here they sat, all three men facing towards Mecca, each with a small cone-shaped pile of sand beside him, a symbolic representation of water which was so scarce and could not be afforded.

The pillars were more of a spiritual healing and way of life which included ones declaration of faith, five compulsory periods of daily prayer, the observance of Ramadan, the offering to charity of a portions of one's wealth, and pilgrimage to the holy land of Mecca during one's life; the five periods of prayer were as follows: at sunrise, noon, afternoon, sunset, and once at night: Salat-ul-Fajr, Salat-ul-Zuhr, Salat-ul-Ast, Salat-ul-Maghrib, and Salat-ul-Isha in respective order, time allotted each prayer and those periods being 10 minutes, 20, 15, 15, and 20.

Being on the road with camels made it wholly difficult to pray as required and so an acceptable alteration was made in accordance with the difficulties of prayer. Sunrise, noon, and sunset were maintained by some of those on the road, the afternoon and night time prayer being dropped, which meant in all reality that for those choosing to travel by day that the only interruption to the string was at noon, a 20 minute period of prayer being adhered to.

Camels could easily be halted and ordered into the sitting position whilst the cameleers absolved themselves for prayer but no time at all was wasted in the ritual. But camels couldn't stand for long with a load and sitting was essential during any rest stop.

Nak was jemadar and for that reason the decision was his to make. Nak refrained from stopping during the day as the heat of the midday sun was no comfort to those permitting their minds to wander whilst static, and secondly; all of his camels were considered as close friends.

## CHAPTER SIXTEEN

The fire was small but was enough to light up the smiles on their faces as they sat with legs crossed and drank of the tea which they had prepared, looking up in wonder to the stars above, not a cloud in the sky.

The night ahead would be cold for them now, considering that there was no blanket aloft the earth, no cloud to trap the warmth, to keep the cold at bay, and before long they would have to draw their knees up to the comfort of their chests, bedding wrapped around them as tight as could be, but for the time being they were content to favour the friendship of one another along with many stories of past, present and future.

The brightness of the stars above was unbelievable, seemingly close enough to touch, more stars than most people would ever see in a lifetime, some winking as thou answering their prayers for peace and brotherly love, for their loved ones back home to be cared for, for sons and daughters to be tended to in a manner fitting a sultan.

And they reflected upon their vulnerability, in particular Shir and Nak, for they were 'old hands', contemplating their apparent loneliness; for they were even without the overland telegraph line which often accompanied them on their journeys to Oodnadatta, running silently above them, over their heads and dreary to look at. There was nothing worse than seeing countless posts being passed, one after the other for miles and miles on end. Such familiarities which brought reminders of civilization were not required when a vast land of sweeping plains, hills and creek lines, harboured the country in quiet solitude, delivering a peace to those that knew the land best. Maybe they were better off without the telegraph line overhead.

The bliss of the evening called for a delightful meal and in that Shir prepared them all something that would set them to heaven and back. Nak tended to the camels once more and saw that most had commenced to wander off some distance from the site where they had been relieved of their loads, and Abdul followed.

Although Abdul was the new man he didn't need to be shown how to handle a camel, Nak wanted to bestow upon him the way in which he and Shir did business and to this he could only pay undivided attention.

These camels were their life's blood and meant everything to them. Even Shir would choose to tend the camels over his new wife for he was a full-blooded cameleer and nothing in the universe could change that. But with duties aside and a full stomach to appease them all, the conversation continued.

Nak fidget slightly and before giving in to sleep decided upon a final story, and he told his story as they sat around the fire as it commenced to die, of a time before Shir and he had met and made a partnership between them. The story was simple and easy to remember for it was always easy to recall the viciousness of some Aboriginal people, succumbed to all matters of evil doing, inflicting the most heinous crime against their own simply because they didn't wish to partake of the celebration, turning down the opportunity to hold a newborn close to heart and with a smile upon the face.

There was an Aboriginal man. The Aboriginal man looked down within the eyes of the newly born girl, another mouth to feed, and of the wrong sex. A boy was wanted by the man, a boy to be moulded in likeness to himself: which is good enough reason in itself for him to be denied his wish for he was a cruel man and everyone knew it.

The disgust upon the man's face told the story within his head, told of his feelings, betrayed his very connection with the one that he should call daughter.

He picked her up by the feet and bashed her hard against a rock, caving her head in, splattering brains over the wife as she watched, tears filling her eyes like the water of a tap fills a bucket, the tears falling in one continuous stream, the hurt within her being heard far and wide. The sadness upon her face could not be denied the feelings of mounting sorrow within a bystander.

The man then took the body of the baby, thrashing loose of the mother's clutching, the mother wanting to hold the dead child one more time, wishing to hold the murdered flesh and bone that was hers and hers alone.

The husband scolded her and kicked out hard before disappearing out of sight and into a creek line where he built a fire and threw the body into it. And here is where the manner of his evil made its final play, for the fire didn't hold and died like the child, and many dingoes came in to tear the lifeless body apart.

How did the cameleer know this, how could he be sure? It was the story told by a friend, a man who had stumbled upon the scene of the feeding when looking for firewood, and the story of the man having bashed the baby's head in by bashing her against a rock was delivered to his ears by a friend of the mother, a witness to the tragedy who was searching for food.

Abdul wasn't sure of the accuracy of the story but couldn't see why he would be lied to. He had seen little in respect to Aboriginal life and even though what he had seen wasn't pleasant it was all too much to think of these people as unforgiving murders; yet it had happened.

With the final story told and minds in a spin over what had been passed between them, it was time for sleep. And with sleep the dreams of the future and past lay visit upon them all, and in their own different way. Shir dreamt of his wife, Nak of his military duties in Afghanistan, and Abdul dreamed that he had wings of gold and flew over the Mungerannie Gap without a care in the world.

## CHAPTER SEVENTEEN

They slept heavily that night.

When morning broke it was met by three men, all three having woken and stowing away their blankets, each in midst stride of his duties, be that packing away the camp, gathering the camels, or simply checking the stores to ensure none were damaged and that all seams on the sacks were intact and not torn.

The sounds still penetrated all around them but they were of a different language, coming from right across the desert and just during sunrise – the break of day. This was around the hour of morning when most are rubbing their eyes for forgiveness, and the last hour before the blazing sun once again beats down upon the earth without remorse. It is a time when birds, insects and frogs in their multitudes voice their presence to the world, ever more so before a storm fills the air and releases a deluge upon the earth.

Other sounds can also be heard from far away, including storms that bypass the area a hundred miles away or more. It is a time of great solitude where the men are kept busy, where time is of the essence and there isn't a minute to spare.

Breakfast, of all things, is a hurried affair for there is much work ahead of them before the string is ready to continue with the move northwards.

## CHAPTER EIGHTEEN

The camels are relatively easy to find, the bells around their necks giving them away fairly easily.

They were within a half mile of the campsite when Shir fell upon Chocolate; the camels had quite obviously had a good night's sleep and had partaken of a good sized meal prior to slumber and another on waking with the morning sun. Shir could see it even from a distance that they were one and all, well-nourished and ready for work.

The camels were brought in, each following the lead of Chocolate, like good soldiers following their leader's orders as laid down.

Abdul confided in Shir for he didn't wish to look the fool in front of the jemadar.

"I feel the social isolation upon my shoulders and the effect it is having on my mind; it's almost too much to bear."

"Try not to worry on it too much," said Shir after a few seconds, walking along with Chocolate next to him, the bell sounding as each step is taken, all but two camels following close behind, for two camels were currently still at the campsite and content with remaining there for the duration of the night, both pregnant, one much closer to birth than the other.

"I suffered, too," continued Shir. "And I know Nak has suffered. He doesn't speak much of the infliction he has but the expression upon his face is not his friend."

"I feel so lonely," said Abdul with true conviction, the sorrow of his voice coming to air, the remark on Nak's grimace hardly being heard.

"You will get used to the conditions and the lack of community whilst attending the caravan, and when in Marree you will find that the support offered by everyone around is enough to help you progress from one day to the next. But believe me; you won't be spending too much time in Marree. From the day you arrived into our arms, as employee and friend, you said farewell to the rudiments of civilization. We support one another now, for all time."

"I miss my wife... my family," said Abdul.

"I understand, as I'm sure they do," said Shir. "We must all do what we have to do in order to survive. It is unfortunate that your sacrifice is more than what most must suffer in order to get ahead in life. But take my advice: think less on this, your predicament, than you do. You won't survive if you keep thinking about it."

"What else is there to think about when on the road for days on end, if not of our predicament?"

"That is the hardest question to answer for everyone is different; we each have a different mind. I cannot answer your question, Abdul."

"Then I shall find the answer for myself."

"And maybe that's the answer," said Shir as they made final approach towards the campsite to see Nak standing there and watching them as they drew closer. "Set your mind free of the shackles that inhibit it and cast your thoughts far and wide, but also... consider everything that is around you, look at every detail, take in all there is to learn. I can't tell you any more than that, I'm afraid."

"Thank you, Shir."

## CHAPTER NINETEEN

The loading of the string was a basic reverse of the unloading of the camels.

Each camel knew its place by smell and sat behind the pack saddle that was to be placed upon it, and as the stores were already placed into bundles, strapped and bound together tightly, they were more easily tied into position upon the backs of the animals.

Shir reached for his soldered canteen of iron that sat to one side of the camel near the rear of the string, a reservoir of drinking water that sat snugly against the girth of the camel.

He took a handsome mouthful of water before returning its plug.

The string was now ready and with bells and hobbles removed, and nose pegs attached, the camels were given the order to stand.

Each and every one of them stood on hind legs first and once straight the front legs opened at the knees, forequarters raising a little, pushing forward onto one front leg at first and then the next.

Nak looked around and saw that the campsite was indeed cleaned of all necessity and that the string behind him was ready to move off with Shir and Abdul in position. This was their second day of many, another eight to ten hours of walking ahead of them; a long stretch of time to contemplate.

So they stepped off, one foot in front of the other, setting themselves upon their journey of a day's march, taking the seconds, minutes, and hours in their stride, the accompaniment of flies ignored as much as the heat of the sun and miles upon miles that mounted behind them.

Nak knew several short routes that the string could take, cutting the trip short by up to several miles a day, making an effort to keep from the main track used by horses and bullocks, for most of the white men of the outback, when on duty and making money from carting supplies here and there, were not very friendly and were prone to slinging abuse, rocks, and generally causing havoc: but in all fairness the extent of abuse was usually kept to a minimum.

At one particular part of the move to the north a segment of track was favoured above all others as it provided better means for which to save time on the road, and it was here that Nak saw a familiar sight coming towards him as the camel train continued.

Chocolate looked up ahead and voiced his opinion. It seemed that he well knew the silhouette of the man and wagon to his front, even at such a distance as confronted him. The sight, however, confused him a little, for the last time he saw the man and wagon they were on another part of the track, and that was a long time ago.

Nak gave warning to the others behind, "Missionary!"

Abdul looked from front to rear and saw that Shir had heard, for he gave a little wave.

Abdul had no idea what was meant by the call but took it to be a warning. The only thing he knew of missionaries was their unsavoury voicing of opinion when it came to God and the son which he delivered unto the world.

Brother Ernest Jacob could be seen up ahead and approaching their slow and tedious move towards the north, the gap between them closing. He had a bullock team under his control and was happy to walk beside them as the Afghans walked beside their camels; it seemed, therefore, that Brother Ernest took as much liking to his bullocks as the cameleers did their camels.

Nak made mention of the Brother as he approached, calling out to Abdul that he was of the Christian religion and a very good man who could be found on the road almost every day of the year, walking his team to and from Port Augusta, supplying the mission at Killalpinanna as required by their service to God. But the endless journey across the desert was now a thing of the past for Jacob, for the train at Marree meant that Brother Ernest had far less distance to travel.

Killalpinanna Mission was first decided upon when the missionaries first arrived upon the land on 31st January, 1867, some three and a half months after first setting out from Langmeil.

Nak considered the move he must make in order to allow plenty of room between the two parties, and although in his familiarity with the bullocks he knew them to offer little aggression or upset towards the camels in general, he still wished there to be a healthy gap between them as they passed each other on the track.

Killalpinanna was not too far ahead, just 25 miles south of Cooper Creek. The out-stations, Kopperamanna and Etadunna, were incorporated into the establishment of the Bethesda Mission, a lot of time and energy being spent on the erection of a post office, church, school, four houses, two store rooms and a dormitory for both boys and girls, and on top of this there was the police station which, after being relocated to Kopperamanna, provided the essential law and order required by the isolated region.

By this time the missionary was passing Nak and a friendly nod was exchanged between the two, Brother Ernest familiar with Nak's grimace and Nak, too, well-adjusted to the man's sermons as he passed, even if beyond understanding.

"May God be with you, brothers. Let him build an altar within you all, a church for which to heal your souls of the savagery enlisted by your beliefs."

Nak understood little of what the man had said as usual, mainly due to his accent, and replied the only way he knew: "Allah be with you."

The name Allah struck Brother Ernest hard but he hid it, as usual, behind a soft and mellow smile.

Two friends, or bitter enemies, showing each other that civilized people could live in harmony; if only for a brief moment. And within minutes the bullock team and their master was gone.

## CHAPTER TWENTY

The days continued to fall behind them until they came upon Cooper Creek.

The crossing was endowed with a 3.5 mile expanse of floodplain, dreary to say the least, but to be compared so pessimistically with the other aspects of the Birdsville Track was beyond contemplation for the entire length was sodden with that tedious plodding along, one foot after the next; but the first call of duty was to cross the flowing waters of the Cooper.

The line of trees on either side of the Cooper were quite prominent and made for a good home to the fishes, birds and amphibian life that remained close by the life sustaining waters. Shadows cast upon the reflective surface of the creek gave it a life of its own, dancing shades of colour flickering upon the surface as the waters passed by at a slow and leisurely pace.

The camels would, without a doubt, have smelt the water from when before they woke for the day's walking and the only considerations in deterring the camels in having tried to advance upon the creek was the restriction offered by hobbles, the fact that they'd only recently (several days before) been provided ample water at Marree, and that they knew they would be passing this way as was the normal procedure on this route. But one thing other than all else was known by the camels before they even stepped foot upon the cool approach to the water's edge and that was the fact that the cameleers were not going to stop for a drink.

Nak knew that if the camels were to be provided time to water that the training of years past would be going to waste. Camels were hard workers but got lazy when men got lazy. The Europeans suffered most of all by camels that couldn't go three days without water, simply because they were provided every ample opportunity to fill up when given the chance.

The camels' water intake allowed them to go longer distances without the need to replenish themselves. Where the strings were trained to go without water for greater stints of time, they did so; the camels were quite capable of going up to ten days or more without water.

It was a sad fact that camels tended to by white colonists were spoiled, for the better use of the word, by being allowed water at any given opportunity, in particular where exploration of the interior was the call to duty of the men that lead them. No one knew where the water holes were and when the next one was to be encountered, but even in reflection of this the whites would see fit to allow the camels water whenever possible. Due to this reason the camels tended to go fewer days before being stressed with the calls for water intake being heard.

A camel would take in anywhere between 16 and 20 gallons at a single sitting and if anything less was drawn then it was a good sign that the camel was being spoiled and not worked to its fullest ability.

Such poor water discipline was dangerous in the case that a waterhole or soak, which was expected to have water in it, turned out to be dry as a bone and in essence prolonged the camels' period between drinks.

A handler, being Afghan or other, needed to weigh his options and knowledge of the land, in particular to take heed to Aboriginal warnings; but the Afghan cameleers stood supreme over all that dominated over the 'ships of the desert'.

During a move towards a settlement where the map was laid at one's fingertips, water was a resource known about, so why endanger the loss of good training and ability?

"We don't stop," yelled Nak over his shoulder as he half turned towards Abdul and continued walking. "The camels will drink if we stop for too long but the need is not present; we also have plenty for our cooking needs."

"It looks like a good place to stop and pray," voiced Abdul.

"We shouldn't change our daily routine," replied Nak. "We must think of the camels; always the camels and then ourselves. Without the camels we have nothing. Allah knows that we are loyal to Him and His beliefs."

"Water is for the weak," added Shir from behind, "and we are not weak."

Camels were a most remarkable animal and there is one solitary thing that stands out most about them... when standing beside a horse they are like giants.

A good camel can be eight to nine feet tall to the height of its hump where the middle of a horse's back will only come to a man's head or chest. This aspect of the camel rarely provided their handlers with better visual options during a supply run because all cameleers walked beside their camels, never upon them, but where space was available and a river needed to be crossed, any white man given the opportunity to ride upon the back of a camel could see the advantages immediately upon entering a river.

The waters of a river would literally soak all that a horse carried upon its back, which included the legs and waist of the rider, whereas riding upon a camel offered greater potential for avoiding getting wet in the same circumstance, for the soles of one's feet would barely be touched by any moisture at all.

Another aspect of great worth was the camels' ability to portage supplies, not just to pull but to literally carry upon its back. A very strong and sturdy camel could carry up to 960 pounds in weight, much more being possible but not desirable, in particular over long distances (600 pounds being a modest benchmark), which was vastly more than a bullock or horse; and even then further weight could be added once the animal was stood on all fours, but rarely was the beast of burden subjection to such pains. Such an advantage proved priceless during river crossings at times when white explorers crossed the land from South to North or East to West.

Pulling a wagon was uncommon amongst the Afghans but others trying to attract a good wage from settlements and mines would see the labour of bullocks used to less effect than a team of camels; in effect the cameleers proved time and time again their superiority in regards to delivering supplies and merchandise, in good keeping with restriction to times, and able to handle the animals with the care and respect that was necessary in order to draw fullest capability from them. And here, once again, a wagon, unless built with height in mind, was subjected to getting quite wet.

There was one other important factor that was praised with great ovation and that was that a camel string could do in two weeks what a bullock team might do in a little over a month: the comparison was simply too daunting to even consider the use of bullocks, but yet there existed the urge to employ them.

Nak and the others continued on alongside their string, neither worried about getting their feet wet nor replenishing their water bags or iron canteens, although Abdul couldn't resist the opportunity to reach into the water with his cupped palm and draw a little of the freshness from that which was offered.

The water cascaded down his chin and neck but also the inside of his throat, the cool and loving freshness like luxury he couldn't believe. It was like being in heaven, and even without the seventy-two virgins permitted each man, the water would have been enough.

Within minutes the string was across the creek and the camels were brought to a quick and temporary stop.

"Check the nose pegs, Abdul," advised Nak. "Sometimes they get broken by the camels in the water."

"Mine are all okay," advised Abdul.

"Mine too," said Shir.

"Good," and without second thought or reflection, Nak turned again to face the north and ordered the camels on.

## CHAPTER TWENTY-ONE

Not far ahead was the Natterannie Sandhills, yellow ridges of its descriptive name filling the scene to their front, a wedge-tailed eagle then caught Abdul's eye, who looked up at the outstretched wings of fortitude as the animal glided high above, seeking a meal in which to feed itself or its young; even though it was a little late in the year for fledglings. The bird was huge, black and long, a diamond-shaped tail with a band of tawny brown across its wings and a chestnut nape.

This was eagle country as far as Abdul knew from his little experience of the country, but he did know that the eagle circling up above was attracted to steep hills, gorges and peaks, and no sooner did he see the bird, and it vanished without a trace, falling out of sight behind a hill not so far away.

Abdul felt like asking a question of Nak, about the wildlife, about his experiences in Australia, but quickly felt the better of it for they would have plenty of time at night when seated around a campfire and drinking tea with their main meal or a little damper. Talking now would do little but dry the mouth more than it was already and expend valuable energy over no better defence than to help keep himself occupied.

It was a wonder in itself, the minds of Nak and Shir. Many hours a day, many days a week, many weeks in a year; year in and year out. What was to occupy a man's mind during such extended lengths of time where there was nothing to do but plod alongside a string of camels, knowing full well that at the end of the day you had to suffer the same burden the following morning and the morning after that.

But Abdul also considered the alternative, living in Afghanistan and doing little else than he was doing right now, where boredom of a simple task could quite literally rattle one's mind into thinking he was insane, even if partly so.

Australia was better than Afghanistan, but only just. The fortune he was to make was a long time coming and the reality of the life he was leading, right here and now, was that there was no fortune to be made, unless your name was Faiz Mahomet of the Durranis or Abdul Wade of the Ghilzai.

He considered, too, the man he had come into contact with; Jehangir, Nak's friend in Port Augusta. He somehow felt as though in debt to the man for Abdul knew deep down, even with so little time in country, that falling into employment with Nak and Shir was nothing less than a blessing. He had good company, a stomach full of food, and a job which offered consistency in pay, so long as they maintained good relations with all they came into contact with.

Abdul pitied the unemployed, those in long lines back at Port Augusta, where men would sell themselves for practically nothing. It was a shame, a disgusting shame, that the men of Afghanistan should be so poorly that they needed to grovel upon the soil of the earth in order to sustain their miserable lives. For some the trip to Australia was a living hell; but there would always be the fortunate few.

A man made his life from what was to be had on offer, and should never take what was on offer to make a life, for such life would often be unrewarding. There was always more fruit on the tree to pick, all you needed to do was to move a few branches; that's what Abdul had done, had carved his own future from stumbling across an offer that couldn't be refused, but only after turning down many other opportunities. He had paved his own path, the way to his own future, and he was currently happy for it, and before he knew it the caravan was pulling up for the night, to take to prayer, and something to eat for both man and beast.

## CHAPTER TWENTY-TWO

North of Mulka, they continued on, and it wasn't long before they fell within distance of Mungerannie Gap.

Mungerannie, as most other establishments, be they a small town or simple homestead, was bypassed for convenience more than anything else.

Nak knew other tracks that could be employed in order to avoid any unpleasantness and that would provide the eye with much more pleasantness than the cold stare of a white colonist.

It wasn't only the Afghans themselves that disgusted many of the white men of this country but the camels too, for most understood that their husbands and sons were going without work because of the camel: but was it the camels themselves or the wages that the Afghan managed to procure from the errands run for settlements and thriving businesses that disgusted them the most?

A majority of the white mans' failures in the outback were not only his inability to maintain a real and proper timescale in respect to the task at hand but more so his greed and hidden ambitions which lead to his depression.

It was shameful to admit that even of those that they aided in regards to carrying wool back to Marree, that a good percentage, in particular the wives – for some ungodly reason – would stare them down, and if a look could kill then they'd all drop dead in an instant: so similar it was to the glance shot at an Aboriginal searching for food or shelter.

It was here that a history lesson was dispelled upon Abdul for this was the place where the Sturt's Stony, Tirari, Simpson and the Strzelecki Deserts met in the quiet solitude of the dry air, any disturbance brought on by sound usually coming from the many types of birds that could be found during the wet season when more than 140 bird species would gather around and bring into the world the next generation of birdlife.

But there was another grand scene that awaited them, for the Mungerannie Gap was closing fast.

It was a sight to appease even the most selfish of eyes, for the beauty of the emptiness came alive on all portions of the ground that they approached, passed, and shrunk into nothingness behind them.

The hills around were a master artist's imagination come to life. Their minds, however, were soon brought back to the reality of life and for the remainder of the journey north further expanses of floodplain could be expected, undulating plains where stones get underfoot and in some places there appears to be nothing around for miles on end but wide open nothingness.

Here, more than anywhere else, the camels feet would have to be looked after and attended to. And they continued on and past Clifton Hill, now eight days into their journey with six to go – or five nights for the optimistic of mind.

## CHAPTER TWENTY-THREE

Just before dark, as the sun commenced to disappear for the night and the air had already cooled dramatically, Nak saw a dingo up ahead, head high and sniffing the air, up to no good and mischief which could easily be calculated; no man needed to be a graduate of a prestigious school to know that a dingo seen at dusk was a recipe for disaster, whether it be a small inconvenience or the meandering mind of something more.

"We have a dingo up front, and we're not far from camping for the night," said Nak to the others.

"Will you shoot it?" asked Abdul.

"Not just yet, but keep your eye open for him when we camp. I don't want to upset the camels by pulling up just now, not being so close to removing the nose pegs."

"What was that?" asked Shir of Abdul.

"Nak says there's a dingo up ahead. Keep your eye open for it in case it comes snooping around camp."

"I see," replied Shir. "Maybe you should tell Nak that we have something more. Slate is ready to give birth soon; she's been grumbling for about ten minutes now."

Nak heard Shir's reply, the wind from behind making it easier for him to hear than Shir.

Nak pulled the string over to the side of the track leaving a little space for any caravan that might come their way at night, for some Afghans preferred to move by night and avoid the heat of the day.

"We camp here," was all that Nak needed to say, for he was

the jemadar and his word was gospel: he gave the orders and read the sermons from the Koran when in the outback running supplies to settlements; he needed little more than to voice his opinion and an order could be deciphered for the betterment of what was said.

Nak could see that the dingo had retreated a little but was still stuck nearer the track than not and so Nak turned to where his rifle lay hidden at rest, tied with thongs to the side of Chocolate.

He undid the ties and prepared the rifle for firing, bringing it into the shoulder after seeing that the string of camels was seated upon the earth and took aim down the sights set for the distance required.

Nak wasn't an accomplished shot and often missed targets that were no larger than a dingo, and so seldom it was that the need arose for the rifle to be fired at all, for the idea of the rifle was to wound an animal in order for it to be killed Al Halal in accordance with their belief.

It was quite understandable that Nak didn't wish to kill for the sake of killing, nor wound an animal that might crawl out into the wilderness to die in agony, but with a calf on the way and the delivery imminent he wasn't about to take any chances, for the price of a camel was substantial enough to provide a more than suitable windfall and provide good reason for celebration.

The other two men stood by their camels that sat waiting to be seen to, ready to be unloaded of their packs and kitchen, Slate slow in reaction to the orders of command and showing great signs of discomfort in the face of what lay ahead over the next few hours. There was no telling how long it would be before the camel gave birth but the walking would have helped bring the delivery along.

Nak aimed the rifle as best he could and with the dingo standing side on and looking directly at him he pulled the trigger instead of squeezing and missed completely the opportunity to hit the pest.

The dingo just stood there as though completely unaware that he'd been shot at, never before having experienced the sound of a bullet from a rifle; in fact, the only movement the dingo made was a sideways glance at the sound made by the bullet as it sped through the air.

Shir laughed and the camels jumped.

"Good shot, Nak," said Shir. "Maybe you should try using your sights next time."

Nak turned to the remark in kind gesture and met the smile with a little wit of his own, "If you bend over, Shir, I won't miss," and turned again to see the dingo standing his ground. "Watch this."

The trigger this time was squeezed gently, the sights having been re-adjusted, and after Nak had opened his eyes from the firing of the mechanism he saw before him a dingo sprawled on the ground. He put the rifle away and stepped off to the carcass.

"Abdul," said Shir, "help me with the camels whilst Nak drags the body away from the campsite."

## CHAPTER TWENTY-FOUR

That night, soon after their prayers had been given in praise of their belief and their tea had been drunk, Slate gave birth. It was of similar colour to its mother and nothing out of the ordinary. The other camels had been set loose on their short hobbles but Slate remained nearer the campfire to tend to her newborn.

The calf sucked upon Slate's udder which was no bigger than a goat's in comparison to overall size.

"Shir," said Nak. "She's your camel. You get a bag made and ready and I'll get some food for Slate. Slate can also be prepared to carry the kitchen; she'll do best at the rear and the further we go the lighter the load will be for her. Abdul, come with me and keep me company."

Abdul saw this as an invitation worth merit, for Nak didn't ask Abdul to 'help me' but rather to 'keep me company'.

Not a further word was said as Abdul stood to follow Nak and Shir set upon getting a bag ready for the calf.

The calf would be spared the anguish of the hard walk ahead – the newborn was needed alive, not dead. It was customary in these times, when a calf was bestowed upon a string upon the road, that the calf should be tied up neatly in a sitting position with its head protruding from the bag and placed upon the mother's back. Shir knew from experience that the mother would look back during the onset of the continuing move northwards, checking that the calf was still upon its back from time to time, giving it a lick if possible and if not then a simple stare of attraction, its head bobbing up and down as the stare was returned.

Slate would continue on knowing full well that the calf was being looked after with her milk, all seven pints of milk from her bladder going to the hungry mouth of the youngster.

The calf would remain in such a position upon her back until they returned to Marree where it would be tended to in good fashion until the next job was ready, and if the job in question required Slate's attendance then the calf would once again be bundled up and taken along.

After weaning the calf could tend to itself and even accompany the mother, attached to another line other than the nose pegs associated with the string until three years old. At three it would be considered old enough to break in formerly and at eight years old enough to be considered as mature.

Nak and Abdul didn't need to take more than a few steps before they came across some food for Slate, spinifex being presented them for easy picking, and they commenced to cut the tussock grass into hand so that Slate could be fed a good quota in order for her strength to be maintained.

Camels ate much of what was found in the Australia bush; Mulga, fifteen to twenty feet of grey foliage with seeds in pods; spinifex (tufts of grass); weeping mulga which was larger than normal mulga bush and rather pretty to look at with silvery leaves, branches weeping as though a willow and usually in reach of a camel's outstretched neck, but out of reach of cattle. There was saltbush which thrived in salty soil and was a good stock fodder, white powder covering its blue-grey leaves... a rather shrubby plant. Herbage like the Sturts Desert Pea was a favourite of the camels where they ate the whole bush including the roots by pulling it out of ground and shaking it free of soil, its seeds dormant during dry times: it was a low trailing plant with hairy grey-green stems and leaves.

There was certainly no paying for fodder, for the outback was like an open market, free for all that could stomach that which was provided free of charge. In a matter of fact the only thing that they really refused point-blank was the eucalyptus.

A camel would grab a branch in its jaws, not its teeth, and pull down, stripping away the foliage of the mulga in particular. There was a small gap between the back and front teeth which made it easier for a camel to take what it wanted and bulls had a small tusk in this gap; thorns were hardly an issue for the camel.

"You've been working hard, Abdul," praised Nak. "How do you find it, here on the Birdsville Track?"

"It's like much of the rest of the country from what I have seen."

"Ah, yes; it doesn't change much in these parts, but the seasons bring enough to provide your mind with a different outlook. Sometimes you can't move because the land is flooded for miles around and at others there will be no rain for many months on end."

"You have experienced this?"

"Yes, Abdul," replied Nak. "I have been here for four very long years."

"And you have yet to make your fortune?"

"Money is hard to come by in Australia. It's hard work being a cameleer. In order for us to keep a job running year in and year we must keep our prices low, too low to make a fortune. Life here is only as comfortable as you make it. It also favours the man who keeps many friends."

"Friends like Jehangir," stated Abdul.

"Yes; that's it, exactly," agreed Nak. "Friends will help you, always. Jehangir was out to look for a young man as yourself, to help me with the camels I have."

"You and Shir must have been working hard these past years with so many camels between the two of you."

"No, no, no, no; not at all," said Nak. "We had another to help us but he met with an unfortunate... accident."

"Is it permitted to tell of this?"

Nak stopped what he was doing and stood up to confront Abdul with the answer.

"He was shot; I was going to tell you," said Nak to an astonished Abdul and Abdul looked over towards Shir who looked over towards them as the words left Nak's mouth. "Shot dead I tell you. That's no lie."

"And why would you lie to me?"

"Listen to me, Abdul," said Nak as he grasped Abdul's arm. "There are very few that you can trust in this country, other than those that read from the Koran. Everywhere you turn you will be met by those wishing to see you dead. Why do you think it is that we stray from the worn tracks, keeping clear of places like Mulka?"

"Tell me," said Abdul.

They moved over to where Slate was lying and placed some food before her, before they too, took a seat upon the desert floor with Shir joining them, an empty sack in his hands being turned into a bag for the calf.

"The rifle I carry is not just for food. It's also for self-defence."

"Have you ever needed it?" asked Abdul.

"Never; not yet," said Nak. "But our friend, the one you replaced, his name was Muschky. He was a very good man, like yourself, with the ambition of becoming a great man, a great cameleer. Do you know that he had this idea in his head that he could become a businessman and recruit many men for the biggest of jobs, working hand in hand with the miners of all description? He wanted nothing more than to meld with those of this country, to help them as best he could. He never had a sour word to say about anyone. But one day, last year and before spring fell upon us, we were on this very track and heading for home. We were near Mulka when a shot was fired and Muschky dropped dead; shot in the head."

"That's no accident," said Abdul. "That's murder. What happened next?"

"Nothing happened, Abdul. I think the shot was meant to scare us but the bullet ricochet off the supplies we were carrying and hit poor Muschky in the head."

"You didn't catch the murderer?"

"No," said Nak in disappointment. "We had little chance. He rode off quickly and had several accomplices with him."

"So why do you tell me this now?"

"When I killed the dingo I was reminded of poor Muschky," said Nak, Shir simply listening intently the whole time, Abdul taking in the story as it was told. "I'm not very good with the rifle and not very good at killing."

"But you were fighting against the British at one time," reminded Abdul. "That must account for something."

"I fear the day that someone finds out about my betrayals; not my betrayals against my country, as you have done, but my betrayal to Australia."

"My betrayal?" said Abdul. "I'm offended by that."

"Abdul, you are our friend and friends speak openly. I mean nothing by what I say. I know you believe you were just, in fighting alongside the British as I am confident in my quest against them, but now things are different. I have a life here and can't go back. If I am found out then that will be my undoing."

"What are you saying?"

"I wish you to carry the rifle, Abdul. You have the right to refuse but I would like to see it in your hands."

"No, that won't happen. Maybe I fought with the British in the past but now I have a family to look after and send money to. You should not hold any of this against me."

"I hold nothing against you, Abdul, but in defence of any

action you might take against a colonist... it would be easier to prove self-defence. I can't prove this, nor can I jeopardise my safety."

"What of my safety?"

"Abdul, I feel I have offended you enough," said Nak. "I am your friend, you must believe me. I needed you to understand my position here, the predicament that could rise from the ashes of last year. You now know the story, you know where I keep the rifle, and you are clear in your mind of your position in this society and ability to prove self-defence."

Shir then spoke for the first time, "It's for you to know everything, Abdul. We don't wish to hide a thing."

"And what of you, Shir?" asked Abdul. "Why don't you take the rifle and kill in self-defence?"

"Because I am a wanted man," replied Shir. "I killed a white man before leaving Afghanistan. I am wanted as a spy by the British." A sad look fell upon Shir for he was revealing something that should not be revealed.

"I should not be telling you this," continued Shir. "No one knows this except Nak, and Nak is a very good friend of mine, better than a brother," and Nak smiled, even in the uncomfortable situation that had arisen. "We could both be treated poorly by judge and jury, myself risking the most. Ah, I see in your eye the questions you have, Abdul, but only one question I will answer. No; that's the answer... you don't deserve to be surrendered to judge and jury any more than us, but it is simply our willingness to go against a conviction that could see us both dead. I will risk it all for a single shot at that infidel that killed poor Muschky, but I might falter in the kill, I might have second thoughts, and any delay in pulling the trigger could easily reap an unpleasant affect upon any of one of us. I didn't receive any great joy from killing the man in Afghanistan; that is the truth."

Abdul was silent for a while as many thoughts went through his head.

"Do you think that killing would be easier for me?" asked Abdul

"In self-defence... maybe," said Nak.

"What you have revealed to me tonight could be dangerous for you both," said Abdul. "Why should you believe that I will look after your secret?"

"For one thing," said Nak, "if you didn't then you wouldn't have asked the question and risked putting yourself in jeopardy, even though there is none."

"Your secrets are safe with me," said Abdul. "But I won't carry the rifle."

"That's fair," said Nak. "I'm happy you know the truth."

"Yes, I now know," said Abdul. "I shall sleep now. Good night."

"Good night, Abdul," said Nak.

"Good night," said Shir.

As the three fell asleep the only noise from the camp came from Slate, who was fast asleep herself and snoring as camels do.

## CHAPTER TWENTY-FIVE

The following days were met by cheerful praise by Nak and Shir who both felt much weight being lifted from their shoulders, but in the same token they also saw the uneasiness within Abdul, a look which dissipated as the days fell behind them.

It was good that the truth was finally revealed, that there were no more secrets to be spoken of between them, and it was good that such had been revealed so far from home, and when so far was to be travelled before reaching the homestead to the north.

The many hours to be endured over the next few days would be filled with thoughts, in particular where Abdul was concerned. He had so much in his head that at one stage he felt quite faint but picked himself up from the depression by taking a good drink of water and by looking around him at the countryside. He was simply amazed by how time had passed since the morning sun had struck the earth and rose clear of the horizon, each day was as seemingly quick as the last.

Before Abdul knew it the darkness of night was almost upon them, on this their last night before reaching the homestead.

The string was permitted to halt for the night as the sun commenced to say it's goodnight to the world and as the orange expanse of beautiful hue stretched across the horizon like a blanket or shawl the camels were painstakingly attended to.

Cicadas as usual, forever in their midst, continued to press their evening joyful song for all to hear, males calling for a mate. It's the heat of the late evening that brings them to life, crying for water and mateship, seeking company as any other creature of the world. Their song is majestic and a delight to hear, a sound so soothing that it helps the men sleep rather than impose many hours and sleeplessness. It's like how a mother's breast can dim the noise of a baby's crying; it had a calming effect, and there was no mystery in that.

But the desert as a whole was a mystery to most, appealing to a majority, and sheer bliss to all by night, for when the sun has said its goodnight the story of the desert commences to unfold, where things unseen are released of the burden of the day's heat where the bright light and searing temperatures of the day do nothing to herald the creatures presence, creatures of the night that come out to play and sing their songs of praise to the world around.

## CHAPTER TWENTY-SIX

The world around Abdul was being revealed; little, by little, by little. The more he saw the more was shared, and this night was no different than any other.

It was important for Abdul to know the whereabouts of nearby towns and settlements, even places where hermits were lodged temporarily in their search for gold, and the police station not so far away was of little exception.

The Diamantina Police Station, put in place not far from the Birdsville Track and just 15 miles south of the Queensland border, was in operation in 1884, a station spoken of and accepted as being established, even before it arrived upon the scene and commenced its role in supporting the wider community. It wasn't much of a dwelling, in poorer condition than the Ghantowns dilapidated shacks of corrugated iron, where corrugated iron could be sought, but was nevertheless duly sanctioned with keeping the peace within the area, collect tax and prevent the selling of alcohol where unlawfully sold. The general location of the police station was provided to Abdul who was advised to seek aid from it should he ever need it.

"Furthermore," said Nak, "is the fact that I'd heard in the air that there might be the need for the station to be supplied with rations, and several times a year at that."

"A good job if it's available," said Shir.

"What will you do about it?" asked Abdul.

"I will consider a friend of a friend," replied Nak. "I know a man in Marree that might be able to sway a contract or two."

"I hope so," said Shir. "Once we get the wool back to Marree from the homestead, we'll be without a job, and we'll be at the homestead tomorrow."

"Unless Ahmad Mohammed comes up with something by the time we have returned," said Nak as he looked at Abdul. "He's quite gifted, in many ways, and can feel the needs of the many and sometimes the few. It's the bigger picture that he sees."

"Who is his?" asked Abdul.

"He works for a man who knows both Abdul Wade and Faiz Mahomet, and for a small the price to be paid for this knowledge – knowledge that is derived from a young women coming of her maturity – this man will release all sorts of valuable information; valuable to us, not necessarily valuable to another," answered Nak as he took a drink of his hot tea.

"It's amazing," said Abdul, "the power that a woman has," and he thought of his wife back at home.

"And Shir can attest to that," said Nak with a smile.

"Ah, yes," agreed Shir, "to think that I am now married."

"Ha, ah," said Nak. "I see it in your eyes. You'd forgotten all about her, hadn't you? Thinking more and more about that pesky camel of yours: Slate and her calf."

"To surmise that I feel more for a camel than I do my own wife is utterly absurd," defended Shir.

"I don't believe a word of it," said Nak and turning to Abdul asked, "do you?"

Abdul stammered, "I, ah... well; to be honest I think Shir has been rather taken in by the delivery of his calf."

"I'm utterly disgusted by you both for thinking so unkindly of my attraction to Slate... my willingness to—."

"Ah, ha; there you have it," said Nak cheerfully, happy that he was right all along. "You feel more for your damn camels then you do your wife; and that proves it."

"Maybe so," admitted Shir, "but a camel can't do the things

that a wife can do."

"That depends on the cameleer that you ask," said Nak as he burst out laughing, followed shortly by Abdul and Shir.

## CHAPTER TWENTY-SEVEN

All three men awoke on the morning of the fourteenth day in tune with those that preceded it, before the sun rose above the horizon and together.

The duties commenced post-haste with Shir preparing the morning meal – conducted shortly after sunrise, their ablutions and prayer – whilst Abdul and Nak stepped out into the countryside in search of the camels that had strayed as usual; all that is, except Slate and the new born calf.

As a dingo had been shot most recently the urge within Nak pestered his subconscious, that he should carry his rifle in case of need, but experience had shown him that this wouldn't be necessary and so he left it behind, wrapped and secured back at camp.

The two men hadn't gone far when the bells from several animals gave them away and they were quickly advanced upon, their silhouettes standing out above the spinifex, the sighting of which might have been missed by the untrained eye for the camel blended in quite well with the surroundings.

Abdul approached one of the bulls of the string and could see the excitement starting to build within him for he was blowing his bladder out, a signal that he wished to mate. The stench of the camel was hardly noticed by Abdul as he tended to it, a big black patch of tar-like-ink sweating from pores at the back of its head, most prolific when bulls were in season; they would take every opportunity to rub it off against anything they could, hoping to draw the attentions of a female.

"A bull is blowing hard," said Abdul to Nak.

Nak was half bent over, looking at the feet of a camel he had a hold of, "Which one?"

"I think it's Joy."

Nak looked up and over to where Abdul was standing, "Yes; that's Joy alright. You'll have to keep him away from the folks at the homestead; they'll not appreciate the smell. The last thing I need is to upset negotiations: I'm trying to ensure next year's contract remains intact and these people get upset rather easily. The man's name is Alfred and his wife is crazy."

"Crazy is a funny name for a woman, is it not?" asked Abdul.

"No; I mean she's simply crazy; her name is Marge, but you must call her Mrs Stapleton, if at all."

Abdul remained perplexed for a moment as he continued with his work, having seen that Nak was going about his business.

The camels were gathered reasonably quickly, just ninety minutes this morning; compared to some days that was a sheer blessing.

Nak reflected upon the ease of the gathering and recalled one time that the camels came in by themselves just as he was about to look for them, led by Chocolate – there was no explanation for it.

"Let's get back now and be off," said Nak. "With any luck we'll be at the homestead well before noon."

## CHAPTER TWENTY-EIGHT

When the homestead came into view the first thing Abdul saw was a reflection of pure picturesque beauty. There was a wooden house and a shed for storage; another for shearing; each with a roof of corrugated iron. A small windmill stood turning slowly as it pumped water from the ground and a dry creek bed sat not too far away.

It was easy to see that the high ground upon which the homestead was erected was chosen well and alleviated all concerns of flooding; that is, for the couple that lived here, not for the sheep which lay in abundance across the expanse of undulating ground, trees of mulga spotted all over.

There were several eucalyptuses near the dry creek bed and ghost gums, too, seemingly lining the lower ground and positioned to take advantage of the water which was offered by the creek during times of rain. It was all too familiar to Nak and Shir, but Abdul was taken in by the savoury solitude of the area.

Abdul could see the farmer – or 'pastoralist' as some preferred to be called – standing to the front of the house and rubbing his hands clean of dirt, a symbolic gesture if any that he was friendly and about to offer his hand in exchange of introduction, but the hand-shaking never came, just a simple nod between Nak and the colonist being shared.

Abdul remained with the string for the time being as Nak stepped towards the tall man in trousers and shirt, the hard work of living off the land evident upon the fabric, stains blemishing what his wife could never clean. He removed his hat temporarily and wiped his brow before returning it upon his head, looking Nak up and down quite briefly before staring at the turban upon Nak's head.

An exchange of words was taking place which Abdul couldn't quite hear and even if he could he doubted that he'd understand any of it. English was hard to learn and only years upon years of working with the white men of the land around would provide any advantage.

Nak used simple words as was his way in order to defuse the pressure of a long-winded sentence from anyone white, for the last thing he wished was to show too much confidence in understanding and then be bombarded with sentence upon sentence of words he simply couldn't piece together.

"So," said Nak, "wool ready, where?"

"Look," said Alfred, the look upon his face showing that he was impatient and couldn't tolerate the lack of English understanding, but nevertheless had a head for business and didn't wish to jeopardise the good relationship he currently shared with the Afghans. "You see, over there beside the house. You take and put on camel after unload."

"Where unload?" asked Nak.

"Over there, in the shed," said Alfred as he pointed over to the dark interior of his storage area. "The same place as last time you were here." But to Alfred these Afghans all looked the same.

Nak could hear the frustration but failed to understand it, for he was simply being polite by ensuring the supplies were unloaded in a convenient spot, for the rainy season would be upon them soon enough and the last thing Nak wished was to unload the supplies upon the ground and then to find that he was required to place them off the ground.

"You lucky," said Nak, forgetting himself and offering conversation where he shouldn't. "No vermin."

"No what?" asked Alfred with a curious look upon his face.

"No rat; you no rat."

"Ah;" replied Alfred. "Yes, plenty rat. There are rats right across this damn country. What do you think; we don't have rats up here?" Alfred was forgetting himself, and the words flowed from his tongue for a bit.

"Unload on ground, yes?"

"No!" replied Alfred in a huff. "Same as last time..! off ground, up; away from wet."

"Okay, I work now," said Nak as he turned away to attend his duty.

As a grower of wool could easily testify, the essence in making a living from conducting such a business was in the actual return of wages for a hard years work and no grower was going to constantly be dealt bouts of depression and stress by having to deal with teamsters and the bullocks, where delay upon delay was the normal outcome, when a good string of camels could do the work under the strong and delicate hands of an experienced cameleer.

Although the camel industry had expanded quite vigorously and it was sometimes hard to find a good job, where a constant flow of work could be taken advantage of, once you were able to prove your loyalty and be on schedule, a job was as good as sealed for the longevity of the unwritten contract which could easily dwarf the decades as they fell behind you. In this, Nak and the others were quite fortunate.

The homestead in which they now attending was enough to provide them with a good wage for their part in the transition of wool from sheep's back to storehouse, and in matter of fact, it was this particular homestead that had seen to it that Nak's current future was set rather comfortably for the beginning of each year to come, but would have to be looked after with delicate hands.

The camels fidget slightly and it was easy to see that they

wished to be watered, but unloading was to come first. Chocolate could be seen, discontent written on his face as he chewed his green cud, hidden within thick lips, awaiting any opportunity to spit, with 30lbs of pressure, half a gallon of filth upon the man's face... it was written in his eyes.

As the cameleers set about sitting the animals and unloading each from the front to the rear, refraining from setting hobbles as the camels were to be watered, not fed. Alfred pulled a thick chain near his tank to allow the water to fill the troughs with their quarry so that each and every camel could be filled.

As the men talked and worked they could see Albert's wife approach one particular package that was wrapped in red cloth.

She turned briefly to see that her only child of three was safely hitched by a single lashing of rope to the post of the home they had come to know, for the last thing she wanted was for a camel to trample upon her pride and joy.

Shir watched as she tended to the article and Alfred carried on his business with Nak most temporarily, for Nak was too busy with what he had to attend to worry about anything else, in particular the farmer's idle chatter, pointing over to the wool on occasion and doing well in his efforts to signify the cargo to be transported by caravan to Marree. Nak wasn't a stupid man and could see without a doubt that that was where the wool was, breaking the invisible borders of the shed in which it was stored, piles and piles of the merchandise ready to be taken away.

Shir continued to watch the woman that hadn't seen him as yet and she unwrapped the article without any thought on the matter, being stupid and half-witted or simply rude and out to cause bitter mayhem.

The sight that was revealed to Shir was unforgettable. There before his very eyes, thirty feet away, was a stack of bacon slivers for the family of three.

Bacon; anything for that matter to do with a pig, was unclean both physically and spiritually. Pigs slopped on the faeces of other animals and such contamination could easily transfer from pig to human.

The Koran forbade the eating of pig, the mullah prohibited the transport of pig and its by-products, and even the eating of a can's contents, where the can was offered unlabelled, was shunned for what it might really be.

"Nak; NAK!" shouted Shir with great terror within his eyes, a display so wrought with horror that Marge Stapleton initially thought that something was wrong with her child.

"What is it!" answered a panic-stricken Nak.

"There, the woman," pointed Shir with wide open eyes and a pointing finger. "Bacon... we've been transporting bacon."

Nak stomped over to Alfred with the grimace upon his mouth twisted out of fashion for his persona, "What this!"

The farmer saw immediately what was the matter and put his hands up in defence, knowing full well that he needed his wool to market on this string or be damned, knowing full well that he couldn't afford another to transport his wool.

"Wait!" said Alfred as he stepped back. "Sorry; me sorry."

"You damn man," cursed Nak. "You very bad."

"No, look... you watch," and with great fury in his face, his lips tight and full of energy, creases forming upon the skin around his eyes and cheeks, Alfred stepped briskly over to his wife and slapped her so hard across the face that she fell to the ground along with the slivers of bacon: It was hard enough to farm wool, and so grateful Alfred was that he held a tract of land upon a small basin which allowed for a reasonable pasture to supply many hungry mouths: such an uncanny site it was.

The woman burst out sobbing, holding the red mark upon her cheek, rubbing her hand delicately where it hurt the most, reaching for the bacon as it lay upon the ground. Alfred kicked it out of reach, "You stupid bitch!"

Alfred looked back to Nak and the others who were quite shocked by the ordeal and had most temporarily forgotten about the bacon laying there upon the ground. Alfred quickly moved over to the cameleers and all could see the sorrow in his eyes as he displayed great apology for what had happened.

"My wife is so ridiculously stupid; I didn't know of the bacon," said Alfred. "It's finished with now, yes?"

"No," said Nak, sorry for what had been done. "No more work. You do own wool, we go home."

"No, wait," pleaded Alfred, forgetful to whom he was speaking with, his English gone haywire. "I didn't know about the bacon, I swear it. If I'd know about it I would have stopped it in Marree. This should never have happened, you must understand," Alfred could feel the contract falling from his grasp; he needed the money from the wool more than the cameleers needed their wages.

Alfred calmed down a little, "I pay more, little extra," said he. "Pay for five more days on road, you get extra money, pay at post office in Marree," Alfred put his hands up to hold back any interruption. "Look, I get letter and give you. You give post office and he pay much; you understand? You give letter to John Arthur O'Brien."

Nak nodded as he looked around at the others, each glum-faced and not sure as to what they should do.

"No more bacon," said Alfred, "never any more; all finished; never see again."

"Okay," said Nak. "We do... job, for you. We water camels and load wool; we go Marree."

"Oh, thank you, thank you," said Alfred, showing his true face, the anxiousness of his need and the assurance offered, the urgency in which he needed aid. The cameleers now knew that they were in a better position to barter if they wished to do so.

"Ask for more money," said Shir in his native tongue. "Take

from him what means the most."

"No," said Nak. "I won't become one of them. We do job, is okay," said Nak. "Bacon finished."

"Yes, yes; thank you," said Alfred and for the first time he shook hands with Nak, showing his gratitude for what the cameleers were about to do for him.

With sudden forgetfulness having fallen from Nak's mind he turned one final time to Alfred and procured two letters from within his pocket, and with a forced smile he handed them to the farmer. Alfred opened each and briefly read them before giving a final farewell, much appreciative of the letters which required no reply.

## CHAPTER TWENTY-NINE

With the camel string watered, loaded, and ready to move by mid-afternoon, the cameleers decided on making way for a waterhole that was known to be situated just off the main track of Birdsville. The homestead had provided water for the camels but it wasn't enough. Maybe it was a part of the farmers mean streak to see the cameleers put out, but this consideration was soon waived for Alfred required the wool back at Marree as soon as practically possible and could not afford to delay them.

The string was made to stand and the march back to Marree commenced, each camel carrying four to five large bales of wool. They would remain loaded for the short stop at the watering hole and continue a little further so that they could keep away from the main flux of mosquitoes that were prone to inhabit such places.

The waterhole was a delight to see and something that the camels took good advantage of, neither entering into the water nor rolling in it, simply standing upon the edge and drinking politely as did the men – it was more of a billabong than anything else, but was not part of an anabranch.

A water fowl was then seen as it took off into thicker scrub, away from the intrusion upon his haven, water lilies and hyacinth catching the men's eyes, a wonderful sight if ever-one was seen; it put the picturesque homestead to shame. Abdul hadn't seen anything like it for many years and Nak cherished the moment for the never ending bleakness of the desert put much strain upon his shoulders; Shir saw the true nature of the waterhole and what it had to offer... more than just water.

The waterhole was far from dry and there would be little semblance of anything so sublime on their return journey; this they knew from experience. So it was for them to take the time now to water the camels and finish with the contract for another year, each man feeling some regret over the episode with the bacon and the debacle that was suffered.

A little further on and their camp was erected, sleep sought with more silence than normal dominating the scene. The camels were left on short hobbles as usual but this night they seemed to remain close to the campsite, the rest at the homestead and their intake of water holding back the pangs of hunger.

It was just before the blankets were put to good use that Abdul went over to a large piece of wood upon the ground, to be used on the campfire. It was unfortunate indeed that he should be bitten by the scorpion, the small creature of the Australian bush being interrupted by this intruder from a foreign land. The upturning of the wood had disturbed the solitude and therefore a welled amount of fear for the unknown burst its banks from within the arachnid.

It lashed out at the little finger of his left hand that was so close... too close for comfort, the smell of the flesh easily detected but unknown. Such an unknown danger with the ability to upturn a home was an invader which required killing and so the scorpion plunged his stinger into the finger of Abdul who retracted himself from the predicament in such shock that he missed the opportunity to see what it was that had bitten him.

He cradled his left hand into chest and slowly revealed the damage to himself, moving his right hand away and then looking down upon the redness of the sting.

Abdul was lucky in a way for he was strong and young; too old and or frail could have meant a prolonged death with much agony when in the outback and without aid, but death was so seldom seen that it was rarely, if ever, raised as a concern, but Abdul wasn't free from the encumbrance incurred just yet.

The pain was throbbing and grew from bad to worse very quickly and the fear that welled up within Abdul was too much for his mind to decipher, hence his panic overflowed and he went running to Shir and Nak, stricken with pandemonium.

"SHIR! NAK!" he screamed as he approached the campfire, the two men standing up from upon the ground, initially lost in bliss, enjoying their tea and looking up to the sky as the stars revealed themselves for the world to see once more. Now they were nothing less than very worried.

Abdul saw the silhouettes of the two men and his panic subsided slightly.

"Nak! Look; I've been bitten," scrambled Abdul, of an explanation for what had happened. "Over there, by the wood, where the ground... it was under it and... look at my hand."

Slowly, Abdul pulled his affected finger from the security of his clench.

"Move closer to the fire, Abdul," said Nak with a slight sense of urgency, fearing that it might be a snake bite.

"Strange it is," said Shir, "but not a snake bite."

"No?" said Abdul.

"No," concurred Nak. "It's a scorpion sting. Look, you can see that it lacks the puncture marks of a fang... the redness is clear and no venom upon the surface of the wound."

"Are you sure?" asked Abdul. "How do you know? How can you be so sure?"

"I've seen bites before, Abdul," explained Nak. "Plenty of men have been bitten and then died by the viciousness offered from a snake. You have to be careful not to step on them during the day. But this is night; you see; past dusk too late for snakes to be out in the closing cold."

"But it hurts so much," confided Abdul with the pain of the

bite scribed upon his face, his eyes seeking compassion without his knowing it.

"There's not much that can be done, I'm afraid," said Nak. "This pain will be with you for some time now, but I've never seen a man die from such a wound."

"No?" asked Abdul for some clarification, wishing to be assured of his safety, looking for the word 'not dead' to be ushered to him.

"No," said Nak, "never have I seen anyone killed by such a thing. You'll have to suffer the pain, I'm afraid, and that's not a nice thing to have to say."

"Will the pain last long?" asked Abdul.

"Maybe tomorrow you'll feel better," said Nak.

"Or the day after that," advised Shir, trying to ease Abdul's concerns, but only managing to escalate the idea that there was much pain to be suffered over the coming days.

"I won't sleep well like this," said Abdul. "I don't wish to shy from my responsibilities."

"You can try and look after the kitchen; if you can, Abdul," advised Nak. "Both, Shir and I, we will take care of everything else, even laying your prayer mat out when it is time. Only do what you think you can do and never shy from requesting help."

"You must promise, Abdul," said Shir. "Say you will give warning to us when you are troubled by the work you do."

"I shall," said Abdul and he smiled with the comfort of the thought that he was going to be okay after all.

The men soon found themselves bedded down for the night with the fire between them stoked and piled sufficiently, the camels going about their business, whether that be feeding or sleeping, though mostly sleeping. As for Abdul, he suffered much that first night but the worst was to come, for the pain only increased over the coming days and would not go away.

## CHAPTER THIRTY

The next day revealed much unpleasantness, in particular for Abdul; the gathering of the camels also took longer than usual, and was an occurrence that Nak just couldn't figure out; normally they were much easier to gather but today several more hours was spent conducting what was considered to be the normal routine.

Abdul had managed to put the kitchen away before Nak and Shir returned, but had refrained from placing it upon Slate. Slate had been doing well as the kitchen camel and didn't seem to mind being shuffled in the order of march by being placed to the rear of the string.

Abdul stood up gingerly so as not to knock his hand, his finger held against his chest, being in much pain, protecting it as best he could. The putting away of the kitchen had been a choir for him but with the extra hours spent in gathering the camels Abdul seemed to have had more than enough time to carry out his duty.

"I was becoming worried," said Abdul to Shir and Nak as they led Chocolate in with the other camels close behind. "What kept you?"

"The camels were dispersed over a wider area this morning and growling more than normal," said Shir. "Not many were eating... they seemed to be looking for something."

"Maybe they were looking for each other," said Abdul.

"You'd be surprised how silly that is, Abdul," said Nak. "The camels can hear the difference in the bells around their necks. They know, believe me; Chocolate wouldn't be hard to find.

When a camel wants something bad enough, he'll get it."

Abdul smiled and turned to his handy work, seemingly proud of what he had accomplished, having carried out his task in more pain than Shir and Abdul could ever realise.

"Good," said Nak. "We'll sit the camels and get them loaded; time is running out and the day is growing old."

They smiled again and Abdul's expression painted a severe warning for the others to see, his face lighting up, the eyes within his head opening wide as though he had suddenly seen a ghastly image.

"What is it, Abdul?" asked Nak as he turned towards the direction in which Abdul was looking and there before him, upon the horizon and approaching fast, was nothing less than a foreboding sight which needed no deciphering.

From north to south, across the entire expanse of the sky came a darkened mass of billowing red sand. It was a sandstorm of the likes Shir and Nak had never seen in their entire lives and they had little more than seven minutes to react before it was upon them.

Sandstorms were not that frequent but were dreaded by all that suffered them, for what they delivered was anything from much lost time to several days of misery.

The large dark cloud of sand that approached from the horizon just kept rolling towards them, great billows of surging force that seemed to literally roll over the ground towards them, mushrooming balls powering on and quite unstoppable.

The sheer terror for all those that witnessed a sandstorm was nothing compared to what was now approaching the three of them.

A sandstorm could last for such short periods or blow for hours on end, it was impossible to tell as it bore down upon them.

"Quickly, Shir, get the shelter from the pack saddle, put it up over there next to the mulga tree," ordered Nak. "Abdul, get the water and some biscuits from the kitchen, we don't have much time; quickly now."

The men rushed to their tasks and Abdul aided Shir after seeing to it that the calf was untied from the sack near its mother, giving it free reign to wander off as it needed to. Shir looked over and saw what Nak had done as he unrolled the shelter, a tarpaulin more than anything else, the most expensive commodity they could afford, the next best thing to a tent, but its size was only enough to protect them during times of inclement weather, not large enough to sit in as though one might wish to sit beneath a spacious tent and cook a meal whilst the night passed them by. No; it was nothing like that; it was nothing short of a very large blanket made of coarse material, used to shelter them from the rain.

"Nak!" jolted Shir for the jemadar's attention. "Tie the calf to Slate, keep them together."

Abdul froze for a split second and then did as Shir had requested, placing a cord between mother and sibling, nose pegs set aside. It was then that Abdul reflected upon Shir's request. There would be no need to tie the calf to the mother unless the storm was to last for more than a day. Was there something in Shir's foresight of what was to come? Nevertheless, Nak was extremely grateful that the camels were not yet loaded.

With the camels quickly forgotten and the shelter briskly erected, it representing nothing more than a small collapsed tent, the centre tied fast to a branch of the mulga and the sides pegged down as best could be achieved, the men took their biscuits and water to the dark interior of the new home, crawling under the shelter on the side facing away from the approaching storm.

Shir looked up again to Abdul, further advice to flood from his mouth, "The Koran! We need it."

Abdul was the jemadar and knew precisely where it was

stored and how best to retrieve it with the minimum of fuss, so without further ado he crawled back outside as the edge of the storm hit him with full force whilst the other two felt the impact of the storm hit them, too, the sides of the shelter pushing against them and conforming to their body shapes in rough fashion as they sat there, the canvas sheeting held upon their bodies by the force of the wind which wasn't about to relent.

For Nak, who had experienced less savage storms of this nature, the experience was terrible. It was as though a blanket had been cast upon the world, it turning from day into night, the cloud of black engulfing him and everything else for miles around, vision denied as a means for which to sense direction, Nak relying on his common sense and basic wind direction to calculate his position and that of the camels, of which all were laying still with their heads away from the grains of sand that pelted their hindquarters

If the camels were moving it would have been a different story, in particular if the wind was less savage and lasted for a short time, for the camels would continue on their way, following one another as each is connected like the cars of a train, the lead camel and cameleer leaning into the task and continuing the move forward, the cameleer unable to see but the feet feeling the way. The camels were a little better off, for camels would simply close their nostrils and breathe through the slit formed where the nostrils met, hair filtering sand from the air as they breathed. The camel's eyes were also fifty percent opaque and so in a less severe storm were able to negotiate their way reasonably well.

But the severity of this particular storm was obvious from the onset and Nak experienced its savagery first hand as he fondled his way from camel to camel, looking for Chocolate and his sacred Koran, the book which meant so much to him and his comrade. He could feel the stinging of the grains of sand as they lashed out upon his body and in return all he could do was to try and keep his head low and in full gear, making sure not to lapse in concentration, not for a single second.

The noise was also quite deafening and seemed to get worse as the storm wore on, whether it was because it was in fact getting worse or because his ears were being deafened by the delivery of the screeching wind as it lashed out its evil upon him.

He felt around each camel's body, leg and neck, seeking out the one he needed, his fingertips doing the hard work for his eyes, the lids of which were beginning to waver. The pressure of his eyes being held shut against the pelting sand and other debris was commencing to take its toll, and before long Nak was starting to feel the pressure of quitting what he had started until he fell with great relief upon the lead camel and the compartment which held the leather bound book of his.

The book was secure between his fingers and now was the time for him to return to his comrades.

He was now more than ever forced to remain upon the ground crawling, making his way back to the tent foot by foot, hoping with his entire might that he was going the right way, the single and most important of all the factors that offered themselves to him being that the direction of the wind was known and computed.

It was then, as he began to question his progress back to the others, that he considered whether or not the wind may have changed direction on him, even slightly. If it had then he'd never find his way back to the shelter.

All he could do was press ever on, trying to keep a mental track of the distance he was covering as he searched the tent out.

He screamed at the top of his lungs for Shir and Abdul to hear him but they heard nothing but the impact of the sound from the storm, the ferocity of the wind almost pushing them over from their seated position within the discomfort of their little hide.

Abdul tried to say something to Shir but he could hardly see or hear his friend; Abdul couldn't even hear himself. He pulled his left hand in for protection and with his left reached for Shir's ear.

Abdul cupped his good hand into a concave shape and yelled into the ear of his friend, "Do you think something has happened to Nak?"

Shir reached for Abdul's ear and yelled back, "No, but even if something is wrong, there is nothing we can do but leave the shelter and crawl around until we find him. If he is lost then he will never be found."

## CHAPTER THIRTY-ONE

Time was taking its toll upon Nak for he'd been in the storm for almost an hour. The thrashing that it gave his body was simply too much to believe for bruising had commenced to accumulate all over him, debris a big factor in what he considered to be the worst storm he'd ever had to face.

He fumbled on in the darkness, his Koran held tight in hand. Of all the things that could go wrong, to lose the Koran would be the worst. He felt for his friends then, the unselfish thoughts that accompanies one when death is considered. He was happy that the Koran was in his grasp for it meant he was with his belief in time of death, and his belief was with him, but his friends would be without it.

He collapsed then upon the ground and the grains of the storm pillared around him, commencing to bury him partially with the landscape of undulating nakedness. He then reflected again upon Shir and Abdul. What need would they have of the Koran? They were alive, not dead; he would be dead, not them. Buried alive! Would anyone find him? Would his final burial place be discovered before he was fed upon by the creatures of the outback, by the winged scroungers that soared through the air far above the surface of the land? The ants, too, would have their way with him, eating every scrap of flesh upon his body until there was nothing left but bone. And what of his secret love for the prostitute of the Ghantown? He would never again be able to lie with Saki.

How he would miss her and the comfort of her soft voice, the warmth of her flesh against his in the heat of a passionate night.

No! He wouldn't allow this to happen, he would do all he could to ensure he survived this ordeal. He had to think positively. Even if he had to remain outside in the storm for its duration he would only go without food for a short time; even water intake wasn't that important, for several hours without water would be fine: he could survive that, surely.

But what if the storm lasted longer? How long could it last? He was beginning to feel thirsty already.

NO! He shook the thoughts out of his mind. He would continue to try and find his friends, if it was the last thing he did, and if he was to grow too tired to continue he would simply find the best shelter possible, like a tree trunk or rock, and curl up into a ball and ride the storm out.

He had a lot to decide upon, but for the moment he had to try and find his friends.

## CHAPTER THIRTY-TWO

Abdul and Shir shared a little of their concerns for their friend, Nak, but in due process figured that he would survive the ordeal, for the storm couldn't last forever. As for them, they had biscuits and water to share and these commodities alone would be enough to keep them occupied.

The thoughts of home now grew within each man, each in his own way, more than ever before. It was like a complicated saga of endless emotions, a roller coaster of fear, apprehension, sadness, and many, many memories of happier times.

The shelter they had erected was certainly not spacious, by any degree. The slashing of the wind against them saw that every inch of space, other than the portion behind them where the interior was protected from the wind, was seemingly sucked from existence.

The two men had moved closer, their backs against the coarse material which sheltered them, a little area to their front made for no other purpose than to deliver them both a feeling of control over the surroundings. Here they lay their biscuits and water, in easy reach. They couldn't see very well at all, it was practically pitch black and they had quickly decided that fire was out of the question.

Every now and again they would share a little conversation but for the most part they remained tight lipped. Their thoughts were on family and home, and Nak. They had no idea how he was coping on the outside or whether or not he'd managed to find shelter. It was hoped that he'd curled up beside a camel or two and remained in the protection of the large animals, but they both knew that he would have tried, heaven and earth, to get back to them with the Koran that he had sought.

In a way it was their own faults that had delivered them this scenario, where two men were without the third, simply because of their need for the Koran. And so they blamed 'it' for the situation and quickly saw the error of their ways, for such a sacred thing should not be accused of delivering such evil upon them.

Neither Shir nor Abdul had requested the Koran be retrieved by Nak, it was Nak's idea to retrieve it, but Shir did bring the object of their obsession into view, it was he, Shir, that had put the idea into Nak's head, had said that they 'needed' it when in fact all that they needed was one another. Shir had dangled the carrot in front of Nak and he had taken the task of retrieving the Koran as being his and his alone.

So Shir sat in silence as best he could and thought about the man that was leader of their treks into the outback and beyond, the jemadar that was seemingly without fault, and was one of the best men that walked the face of the earth. It was only his grimace, the facial expression upon his face and couldn't be moved, that allowed people who didn't know him to think differently of him.

It was of very poor character that anyone should think badly of Nak simply because he looked different than most, in the same way that people perceived Shir, for he was quite ugly, very unpleasant to look at, but had a heart of gold and could never be faulted for who he was and what he represented. Shir was a free man and lived with a free spirit, but followed his belief to the ends of the earth.

Shir was a religious man and it was here in the midst of the storm that he felt the urge to pray to himself for hours on end in order to keep himself occupied, to give him hope.

## CHAPTER THIRTY-THREE

Before Shir and Abdul, beyond their sight, the day had fallen behind them and the dark of the night was being delivered unto the earth. If it wasn't for the fact that the storm was still thrashing solidly against them and their shelter then they would have known about it, they would have known the time of day.

Their biscuits were gone and so was half their water, having been drunk out of sheer boredom, not out of necessity, and it was for this reason that Shir felt the urge to pass water and needed to depart the luxury of the tent for a short time.

Shir cupped his hands around Abdul's ear as Abdul put a biscuit into his mouth and shared with him what it was he wished to do and Abdul was fluxed with sudden realisation that if he'd wanted to relieve his bowels of the previous days meals he'd consumed he'd be in true difficulty.

Shir departed the tent, crawling upon all fours, and Abdul finished his biscuit before deciding that he wanted no more. It would be difficult enough to pass water, let alone anything else, and with that still in his mind he decided to try and get some true rest by lying upon the ground... after Shir had returned and they had the opportunity to pray.

Abdul touched his finger then and the sheer pain of the gentle touch rode up his entire arm. The pain was getting worse, certainly not better, and he was worried for what might lay ahead for him and the scorpion bite. He'd been bitten the night before and the full cycle of a day had passed him by. He could feel the tiredness within him, tiredness which comes with the passing of many hours. He knew the day was over, even if he couldn't see anything of real value from within the shelter that he sat. Twenty-four hours with increasing pain: he would see what the morning brought.

Shir came back into the shelter having relieved himself, a majority of which had ended up running down the inside of his leg. He refrained from saying anything to Abdul for it mattered little, and so they gave praise where they sat and laid down as best they could to get some sleep.

And so, rolled up close to each other, the material of the shelter covering them both, flapping hard against their bodies, they eventually fell asleep.

## CHAPTER THIRTY-FOUR

Abdul woke with a great fright falling over him and as he woke he felt a suffocation crushing him. The pain in his finger suddenly shot through the roof as he jolted awake and he tried sitting up, but his efforts gave little reward.

The stirring of his body against Shir also woke him and together they did all they could to sit up again, the weight of the sand upon the skin of the shelter that covered them making it extremely difficult to move.

The panic within Abdul was slower to subside than with Shir, not because of the pain within his finger, but due to a dream he was having, a nightmare that tore at his fears.

Shir fondled around until he found Abdul sitting there beside him and searched for his ear.

"What happened?"

"I had a bad dream," answered Abdul. "Is Nak back? Have you seen him?"

"He hasn't come in."

"My finger is very bad," said Abdul at the top of his lungs. "I fear the worst. I've never had pain like this before."

"We'll have to have a look at it once the storm clears, but at the moment there's not much we can do."

"What time do you think it is?"

"I have no idea," said Shir in reply. "Maybe I should have a look outside, see if the sand has given way to clear sky."

"The wind is still blowing hard."

"It's worth a try," insisted Shir. "I don't like the idea of sitting here for another day if the outside world is clear and we can see what we are doing. We have to find Nak."

"He would have found his way back in here," said Abdul.

"Not if something has gone wrong," advised Shir as he crawled out into the sandstorm that had continued in its ferocity.

Within seconds Shir had returned.

"It's no use," said Shir. "It's as dark as before."

"What time of night or day do you think it is?" asked Abdul

"I'm still tired so maybe it's night; I also feel a little chill."

"I'm tired too but the pain is worse."

They continued in their friendly way, the need for each other's company so very important and required. They needed to support each other, now, more than ever.

"I think I need to do something about my finger," said Abdul.

"What, exactly?" asked Shir.

"I think it needs to be removed."

Shir fell silent for a few seconds before deciding that there was nothing further to do or say. Both men were silent and they considered the predicament that they were in. They had very little water and no biscuits. He would lie back down again, until the build-up of sand upon him woke him or Abdul once more.

## CHAPTER THIRTY-FIVE

The two men slept on and off for what seemed to be an eternity, sitting up to push the sand from upon them every now and again, this effort alone draining them of all energy.

Abdul had never before, in his entire life, ever had so much time to contemplate his life. He considered the errors of his way, the friends he had treated poorly and those he had treated well.

Friends were friends, and all were of different character. He thought of those that were weak and those that were strong, how each characteristic brought on different meanings in each, how they differed in their perceptions of life and death.

In reality, one was no different than another. They were all friends; they simply had a different perspective on life. Why would he treat one more favourably than the next?

He would, from this day forward, treat each and everyone the same.

Shir, too, was exposed to many thoughts, some which bothered him and others which instilled great confidence within him.

Shir concentrated more on his past, the way his life had unfolded to lead to this day. He had a father and a mother in Afghanistan, both of whom were dead and buried; but nevertheless he reflected upon them and his country.

Had he done the right thing in his fight against the British, his actions as a spy? He had killed a white man and now he regretted it. The long day before Shir now paved his train of thought and within the span of a few short hours he had courageously confided unto himself a promise to never kill another man for the remainder of his life.

And as the contemplations of life continued for them both, the outside world continued in its day to day rituals, where the sun rose and then fell again; day turning into night.

## CHAPTER THIRTY-SIX

It was quite some time later, Abdul not sure exactly how long, but long enough it seemed for him to get enough sleep before the entire world that encased him came tumbling down, the large branch of the mulga to which the shelter they had erected was attached, broke away and smothered both him and Shir.

The panic within each of them in those few seconds was overwhelming. One moment they were able to quite comfortably breathe and get some rest and then suddenly they were woken and being crushed by the weight of the sand upon the makeshift tent.

Both men fought to get out from the mess of the fallen tent and scrambled as best they could for the outside world, losing one another in the process, moving blindly into the storm which hadn't yet appeared to settle.

Abdul could feel the searing pain of his entire arm, now nothing more than an appendage that he couldn't move. He moved around and found the base of the mulga and sat there, covering his face as best he could with the clothing he wore, cradling his arm against the force of the wind to no avail.

Where was Shir, where was his new friend, the one he had come to learn so much about over the past few days. And that's when it hit him hardest. The reality of the situation was that they had been suffering like this for quite some time and his arm was nothing less than testimony of the amount of time that had passed since the storm arrived.

Abdul sat in his misery and looked up, thinking he'd heard

something but not quite sure. And there it was, the shadow of a hunched figure running towards him against the wind, and then the shadow disappeared.

The figure of Shir then collapsed beside him and clarity came once more to the area, a little light to shed some visual aid to the dilemma they were in.

They snuggled together, Shir doing all he could to help Abdul protect his arm, for Shir was not a selfish man; none of them were.

The minutes ticked by and slowly, but surely, the wind dropped away and the sands settled, the surroundings becoming clearer and more easily seen.

All of the spinifex in the area was covered in sand which even now became unsettled and fell upon the ground like tiny dry waterfalls of grain. The sun came out from hiding, away to the west as night commenced to grow. There would be around three hours of light left before night visited them once more; three days of darkness they had suffered and yet there was more to come.

Shir was the first upon his feet as he stood and looked towards the tail of the storm as it moved away and seemed to die. With abruptness he turned to look for the string of camels; what he was confronted by was shocking to say the least but he had expected it.

The wool and pack saddles were strung everywhere, some having moved up to twenty feet during the storm and the camels could not be seen, none that is except Slate and the calf. They were nothing more than two piles of sand, one large and one small, in the same place they had been left, two carcasses ready to be filtered by the food chain to the pores of the earth: in a few days there would be little left of them.

Shir tried with his entire might to listen for the bells of the camels, to try his best in locating them... how far had they gone, were any still alive?

Suddenly Shir turned and saw Abdul sitting there with tiredness in his eyes and the pain of the arm written upon his face. His friend, Nak, was nowhere to be seen.

"Nak!" yelled Shir as he moved over towards Abdul. "Nak! Where are you?"

With a great surge of joy erupting from within him he heard the reply, music to his ears, from about two hundred feet away.

"Here!" cried Nak. "I'm over here."

Shir looked over towards where the sound was coming and he could see Nak's outline emerge from the desert with a single camel following; it was Chocolate. Nak had found himself a little shelter, and although not the best it had served him well, for Chocolate was a true companion.

Shir smiled as the bell around Chocolate's neck swung into action and by the time Nak was just metres from his friend a few other camels could be seen to come out of the desert landscape to join them.

## CHAPTER THIRTY-SEVEN

They sat around the fire and looked one another in the eye, each thankful for what they had been given; this second chance, for it seemed as though death had visited them all but had decided not to cast his vicious spell.

The fire was lit in plenty of time to prepare something good to eat for they all had big appetites, in particular after so many days, and water went down rather fast. They discussed several issues which confronted them, one of which was the camels, for without them they had nothing.

"It's almost dark," said Abdul. "I think it's time to do something about my finger."

"What can we do?" asked Nak. "There is nothing."

"I need to amputate it," said Abdul.

Nak looked from Abdul to Shir and then back again, "Are you mad? Maybe the storm has affected you," said Nak.

"He's right," said Shir. "Something needs to be done."

Nak saw the reality of it all within Abdul's eyes but didn't wish to respond.

"It has to be done, Nak," pleaded Abdul. "I can't move my arm, the pain is unbearable, and I fear that death will be the result if something isn't done soon."

"What is cutting your finger off going to do?" asked Nak, disturbed by the talk.

"It will take away the source of the pain," said Abdul.

"The source of your pain is your arm," said Nak, not too bluntly, "shall we amputate that?"

"I hope not, Nak, but if it must be done, then it must be done," replied Abdul.

"He's right," concurred Shir. "He should take off the finger. I have shared much with Abdul whilst in the tent and I recall, quite distinctly, that a man of Afghanistan, near my village in fact, took off his finger under similar circumstances."

"Yes," said Abdul. "I, too, have heard—."

"We have 'all heard'," interrupted Nak. "That story is very old and has been told many times. Much has been forgotten in its translation and passing from one to another. You can never rely on fables."

"Nak," pleaded Abdul, "look at me; look into my eyes."

Nak did as he was asked and felt the hurt within him, that his new friend had to disfigure himself. Nak had lived with disfigurement for some years now, with the grimace of his mouth the way in which it was. He always received unkind stares from onlookers. But at least Abdul's disfigurement was small and could easily go unnoticed.

"Okay," said Nak. "I'll do it. I'm the jemadar, it'll be my responsibility.

"Thank you, Nak," said Abdul and without further ado the preparations were carried out before the sun disappeared completely, for Abdul feared he wouldn't see the light of day if the injury got any worse.

## CHAPTER THIRTY-EIGHT

Shears... clippers for the cutting of hair whilst on the road... instruments employed for many reasons, cast in rust stains but oiled well and looked after, for such pieces of equipment were quite expensive.

"These will do," said Nak to Abdul and Shir as he held up the shears that were to do the job of cutting away Abdul's finger. "It'll work as good as a knife... they're very sharp."

Nak sat down beside the other two men, a small rock in front of Abdul.

"I'll not use them as I would normally, Abdul," explained Nak. "I'll simply hold the blade over your finger and then hit down hard with another rock upon it," Nak looked him in the eyes again. "It will hurt, Abdul."

"It can't hurt me any more than I hurt already," said Abdul with seeming difficulty. "I can't take much more. Please; be swift."

Nak looked to Shir as he placed the blade over the finger and prepared the rock for its delivery upon the shears, "Look away, Abdul, so you don't flinch. Are you ready with the bandage, Shir?"

"Yes, I am—" commenced Shir as he held it up in display, and before he could finish the sentence, and without any further notice or warning, Nak smashed the back of the blade and Abdul's finger came away without any trouble.

Abdul had been taken by surprise, as was Shir, and Nak was amazed by the small amount of pain that Abdul displayed as the finger came away from his hand. Nak could only think that the amount of pain Abdul suffered was so great that the amputation was nothing more than a tickle, either that or the paralysis was so bad that the pain somehow failed to register with him.

Shir moved hurriedly with the bandage as blood seeped from the wound and secured it in place quite masterfully after a brief pause to allow the wound to cleanse itself of any poison.

Abdul looked upon the place where his finger had been and then to where it lay upon the ground before Nak picked it up and threw it into the spinifex.

"That's it, there's nothing left we can do for you, Abdul," said Nak. "The rest is not up to us. If the paralysis in the arm does not go away and the pain gets any worse then I don't know what we can do."

"My arm will have to come off," said Abdul.

"That will be for some other to decide, not for me; nor you, Abdul," said Nak. "Only a doctor or nurse practising in such things can decide upon the fate of your arm. Our job now is to see you, and the load, delivered to Marree. If your arm doesn't improve then we'll try and find help in one of the other settlements close at hand."

"But your load," said Abdul. "It'll be late getting to Marree."

"Better late than never," said Nak. "Besides, we're already behind schedule and will have missed the train. The shipment will be sent in the next available train."

"Will Stapleton be settled with that?"

"Maybe not, but he knows as well as anyone else that you can't rule the weather conditions; besides, he knows that the wool will be delivered, even if a little late; he'll just have to suffer the inconvenience of getting paid a little less for his wool. He'd not have done any better with bullocks or horses; he knows that as well and we do."

"You are right, or course," agreed Abdul. "I think I'll get some sleep now."

"Yes," said Nak, "you do that. Good night."

## CHAPTER THIRTY-NINE

Shir woke to the sound of a bell, the night very still and the stars out in all their glory.

"What are you doing, Nak?" asked Shir.

"I took Chocolate's bell from him when I tied him up. I thought that ringing it during the night might bring some of the camels home."

"Home," scoffed Shir. "A funny place this is to call home."

"You know what I mean."

"Yes," said Shir, "I know. So what do you intend to do, sit up all night and ring that bell?"

"I'll sleep," said Nak. "As I wake during the night I'll ring the bell and sleep some more."

"I'll help, too," said Shir. "It'll help if the camels return by their own accord."

"Thank you, Shir."

Shir smiled and Nak lay down to go back to sleep and as he drifted into a dream, Shir stood up and looked to the heavens.

The stars were out in all their glory and although the moon was of little help the brilliance of the stars were enough to provide that required amount of light for a search to be conducted.

Shir considered that he was currently the strongest. Although the shelter of the tent wasn't great it was enough to provide shelter from the worst of the storm, whereas, Nak was exposed to its full ferocity. He also considered Abdul and the lack of sleep he had suffered due to the pain in his arm. If Abdul could be afforded sleep then he should be left to slumber.

Shir left the bell where it was because he didn't wish to confuse any of the camels by ringing it and then shifting his position; he'd simply move out into the wilderness and search them out as best he could, using the fire as a guide in the night, for it would be able to be seen from quite a distance.

As luck would have it, Shir came upon the first of the camels within a few minutes; it was heading back to the camp. He took hold of it and led it the remainder of the distance before tying it up, the camel being as weary as the men from the ordeal suffered in the face of the storm.

It stood to good reason that most of the camels would be awake and feeding as they wouldn't have had much opportunity during the weathering of the sandstorm. The natural fodder from around would be enough to provide the camels with a little moisture and a good fill, ready for all the days' work that was to fall upon them all, be they ready or not for a hard day's labour.

Within the first thirty minutes of Shir's expedition to search for the camels he had found almost half of them, and as the tiredness of his efforts commenced to build upon his wearied form he turned back towards the campfire to get some rest. As he walked he fell upon a carcass, a camel dead and decaying, open wounds quite clear; he'd been taken advantage of by some of the wildlife in the area, be it dingo after an easy meal or some bird of prey.

The flesh seemed to move and it was then that he realised that the flesh was alive with maggots.

Shir turned away from the vision of hopelessness and continued to the camp.

## CHAPTER FORTY

Abdul rose the next morning to find the sun making its approach upon them all, with Shir cooking a meal upon the open fire and Nak standing up near the edge of their small camp and looking out over the desert surroundings for any visual sign of further movement, camels that might be returning.

"Good morning, Nak; Shir," greeted Abdul.

"And you too, good friend," said Shir with a smile.

Nak turned upon hearing the voice, his grimace set fast upon his face, no smile evident but softness within his voice indicating his pleasure at seeing Abdul rise.

"How is your arm this morning?" asked Nak.

Abdul moved it around in display, "I think it's getting better. A little walking will do it well, some circulation to get the blood flowing."

"Probably true," said Nak, "but you shouldn't over do it."

"But the wool," said Abdul. "It must get back to Marree."

"We're late as it is, like I said," said Nak. "Any further delay will not alter the price at the depot. Our friend at the homestead was to be paid for delivery by deadline, not lateness in delivery."

"Do you think further contracts will be lost?" asked Abdul.

"No," said Nak, "but he'll try his best to alter the price he pays us for transportation and we'll have to consider accepting it in order to keep the job."

Abdul saw the camels sitting upon the area where the packs had been re-laid in position, "How many camels are missing?" he asked.

"We're missing ten camels," answered Shir, "and three of those have been found dead. I think there's a fourth out there," and he pointed into the distance, in the direction to which the sandstorm had been carried, out into the east. Scavengers could be seen flying around.

"That leaves just fourteen camels," said Abdul without need.

Nak turned on Shir, "They're good camels. They'll carry the load, even if we have to make the days shorter."

"Well... shall we start?" asked Abdul.

Nak stepped towards him then, "After breakfast," said Nak. "We'll commence after breakfast. Just six hours on the road is all we'll do today. This will aid the camels and you, too, Abdul."

Abdul was happy that he'd been considered well by Nak, his arm still a little painful, but the camels were also given much consideration: Abdul was not much more than an equal... or so it seemed, and this dwelled upon his mind: man and camel; one and the same.

## CHAPTER FORTY-ONE

They hadn't been on the road more than an hour when they came upon a sorrowful sight, a small Aboriginal community on the move and in search of food.

The Aboriginal way of life seemed to be in turmoil and growing worse, ever since the Europeans had commenced their colonisation of Australia, and the expansion into the desert regions of its centre was commencing to take its toll.

Times were changing for the Aboriginal and for the better, but it was the people themselves that stood in their own way for improvement to be gained in their everyday life.

If there was one thing that Abdul had learnt it was that the Chinese, Italians, Japanese, other men and women from many lands, as well as the Afghans, had poured into Australia and were doing reasonably well under the circumstances of the times. Sure, many lived in poverty, but for those that chose to work hard and make a living from their opportunities, all praise must go. But there seemed to be one thing that made the difference between success and failure amongst the Aboriginals, whether it was true or false, and that was the availability of alcohol.

Abdul had heard many times of drunken Aboriginals falling over the land that they claimed as their own, even though their Dreaming proved that man did not own the land but was simply a part of it, the land owning man more than the other way around.

There were five men, four women, and six children of

between four and nine years of age, each with something in their hand or upon their shoulder; vessels for the portage of water or for the digging of roots; bags or bed rolls and other utensils.

Several swags came into view and this was followed by the powerful stench of each. The swags were nothing more than rolled up blankets and within the roll of each were things such as tea, dried bread, and cooked kangaroo (the head and shoulders cooked in ashes with the skin still attached, where the juices of the flesh seeped into the blanket). The Aboriginals, too, were unwashed and simply wreaked of odour so powerful that even the camels had a hard time keeping a steady head as they continued on past.

The women were quick to offer their hands for food, asking in broken English for a handout.

"No," said Nak as he passed. "No food; is all gone."

Next in line came Abdul, who also shook his head and displayed an uncomfortable disposition with regards to offering nothing, for like his friend, Nak, he hated to see people of this country go without; but there was nothing for it but to continue on.

He shook his head as he looked down upon the sad faces of the children, two of which also held out their hands, hands that bore the brunt of their way of life. The palms of their hands were nothing more than large scars where several fingers had been fused together, their hands burnt by accident as they wandered around camp and fell into open campfires. It was also quite common to see little children of Aboriginal background stumbling around as they walked, having stepped onto a campfire that had been doused with sand but still very hot, parents of the young ones not doing enough to care for the children in their life. Abdul could only wonder what it must be like to be one of them: out of work, without food or money, drunk and seemingly uncaring, treating children as little more than labourers.

Shir was last to pass the small group and as he did so the cries for something, even small, were pleaded for and reached his ears.

Shir reached into his own pocket and threw one of the women some dried meat, not considering for a moment that the Aboriginals may well have had more than he with the kangaroo head in the swag, for a majority of his own food had been lost to the desert, having broken open and being lost in the wind, sacks of flour disappearing without a trace.

Nak looked behind and saw Shir giving what was his own. Shir met his glance. No words were necessary, Shir knew full well that what he gave was his, that he wouldn't get any more to replace his handout and that tonight he would have less to eat than the other two; but he also saw the reflection of understanding and felt that Nak, too, wished to give.

There was no doubt about it; Nak was the stronger of the two and it was fitting that he should be a jemadar.

## CHAPTER FORTY-TWO

By late afternoon the misery of the past week came to call upon the memories of each man differently, so vivid they were, and no surprise really considering that it had been only a few days since the worst had occurred.

The episode with the bacon at the homestead shone light on the subject of ridicule and poor understanding, where the Europeans and colonists – no matter what they were called or referred to as – simply ignored the trivial aspirations and aspects of Muslim life: what was so common to them was a thing of disgust and mockery to those of Christian belief. In fact, the white men of Australia appeared to accept more, the other religions commuting around, and even respect them a little, though not so influential as that of the Christian belief where men like Brother Ernest Jacob set out with the pure intention of delivering sermons to the Aboriginals of the country. But did the Aboriginal ever endeavour to impose his own beliefs of Dreaming upon the invaders of this great land? To Shir it was simply too much to live with at times. Why should it be for him to openly accept all other nationalities and their ways if not a single one of them was to accept him? What was it exactly that disgusted the white men so much in regards to his beliefs?

The work was hard; always so hard, and sometimes even intolerable. Insurmountable pain must be suffered by some, as it was with Abdul and the scorpion bite, amputation, and feelings of incompetence due to issues with missed family, and his personal responsibilities. Such responsibilities were a great weight which simply couldn't be lifted from within, and it was only due to the pain of his arm that he received a little reprieve from his thoughts on family and home.

But of all the problems that were suffered by all three men it was Nak who suffered the most. It wasn't his lack of companionship, for he had the bought love of Saki; it wasn't the grimace upon his face, for he had the friendship of the community at large which accepted him with open arms; but it was the inability to deliver the wool on time to the Marree station.

It was certainly no fault of his own that the sandstorm had been suffered by them, but it was his reputation amongst those that didn't accept him which mattered. He felt obliged to be on time with delivery for this, he felt, was the only way to secure good relations between the Muslims and the others.

The loss of ten camels, and a calf, was going to have a great effect upon his abilities to perform his duties but he was confident that he would find a way. He had the reputation of good quality and spirit; good understanding of the way life was in Marree and other towns and settlements similar to it. He knew plenty of men from whom he could squeeze a deal in good favour without damaging his natural ability to remain friends. So what was it that was getting into the mind of Nak? It was everything as a whole, the entire weight of mounting misfortune and poor treatment. It was his life in general, not a single episode or emotion but everything combined. He was like a well-built dam that could handle the insurmountable weight of crushing abnormality, but his banks were on the edge of bursting. He was at the end of his tether and he wasn't sure he could take much more before he collapsed into a ball and surrendered himself to death. But for Nak, death would never be an option; he could never surrender. He didn't surrender to the British back in Afghanistan and he wasn't about to admit defeat here, in

Australia. He would defeat and conquer before permitting himself to decay and rot.

So it was these three men, each carved from granite of different solidity, that the future was about to deliver the heinous acts of religious and racial hatred upon them.

By the time they reached Mulka they were still three days behind schedule and the camels were growing weary of the weight being carried day in and day out, many miles per day being suffered over the stretching hours that fell behind them.

## CHAPTER FORTY-THREE

Each camel was carrying five bales of wool, some carrying six, and the three cameleers trod ever on, proud of their accomplishments in the face of misfortune but disappointed in what they knew the future would deliver them in regards to the cost of replenishing stock. A few smaller jobs would be okay to accept but this was a growing country that wasn't prone to quit in its efforts to succeed: And unknown to the cameleers, they were being watched; watched by five pairs of young eyes, and from some distance away.

It had been delivered to the ears of those that watched that the camel string was coming their way and they wished very much to meet it with their frustration of the camel industry and what it had taken from their fathers and families in general.

The five young white men, barely of age to drink or partake of gambling, had lived in Mulka for as long as they could remember, having been brought up on the harshness of the land which was their home and place of great joy.

Each one of them loved the soil beneath their feet, even though they condemned it to hell on many, many occasions, for the flies, dust, ants, snakes, lack of water during summer, and lack of dry land during some wet seasons, were just a few aspects of misfortune they loved to complain about. Each was a comparatively able bodied stockman and had a future which could be well suited to them and a wife. A proud life could easily be scored from what they knew about the land and the industries open to them. As general farmers go they were no different than any other, but they did have the mentality of derangement which is brought on by animals in a pack.

The five young men were tying up their horses in the low ground not far from where the camel train was to pass, a creek that flowed well with water during the wet season and offered much in respect to water for stock at a time when the water tanks were dry and watering holes were little more than dry pans of scorched earth for the weeks before the weather turned from dry to wet.

The young men were known to one another by their nicknames and rarely, if at all, ever used their Christian names. They were Scotty, Snake, Bullock, Horse and Fly; Scotty for Scott, Snake for he was thin, Bullock as he was large, Horse for his appendage, and Fly as he was tiny in stature and seemed to literally fly through the air when riding upon a horse at full gallop.

Scotty pulled a can from the saddle bag upon his horse and held it up for his friend Fly to see, a red label wrapped around it. It was a can of bully beef, an invention of a man from the Booyoolee Station and adopted into the Australian psyche, chunks of beef drowned in gravy, a staple that could not be lived without.

"What do you say to some bully, Fly?" asked Scotty.

"Shut your mouth, you fool," scolded Horse. "Those damn freaks'll hear ya."

"Calm down, Horse," said Bullock as he pushed himself up from his position upon the edge of the creek, relieving his vision of the camel train. "They're still a ways off yet."

"I'm gonna clobber me one of those fellers damn good," said Fly.

"You and what army?" said Snake jokingly, pushing into the side of him with his shoulder, a smile upon his face.

Fly looked around a little perplexed by the meaning; for that's what they were there for, to act as they'd said they would, to fulfil their act of revenge upon the men and their stinking camels.

"Shut up, Snake," defended Scotty, "leave him alone."

"You don't have to defend me," said Fly, puffing out his chest. "I might be the youngest but I can lick those men as good as anyone."

"You won't need to," said Bullock, the eldest, "because I got me-self something hidden away," and with that said he drew out a rifle from hiding, from deep within his bed-roll.

"Where the hell ya get that?" asked Horse with a little panic in his voice.

"It's me dad's rifle," replied Bullock.

"You're not gonna use it, are ya?" asked Horse.

"Why the hell wouldn't I?" said Bullock. "What the hell do ya think I bought it for if not to scare those buggers off our land once and for all?"

"Scare them," protested Fly. "We should shoot the bastards!"

"No, no, no," interrupted Scotty. "You don't want that, Fly. We don't need any trouble with the law."

"What law?" said Snake and he too took a rifle from his bed-roll.

"What the.... What the hell you two doing?" stumbled Scotty

"Look," said Snake. "If you don't want in then go home; but I'm staying. I've had enough of these bastards, once and for all."

"They're just men," said Horse. "Scotty's right, we shouldn't be shooting them. The law'll get us all."

"Look," said Bullock. "The closest police is in Marree. We're not gonna get caught; not unless someone here tells on us; turns us in, maybe."

"Don't look at me, Bullock," pleaded Scotty. "I do what you think is best, but I don't like it."

"It's what they deserve," said Fly.

"I would've thought you had enough sense not to be so... power hungry," said Scotty.

"Hey; he's with us," said Snake, "aren't ya, Fly?"

"Sure am," answered Fly as he looked at Scotty. "Ah, come on, Scotty. Them fellahs have been taking our fathers' work for ages. It's gotta stop."

"He's right, Scotty," said Bullock. "The lines gotta be drawn, once and for all."

"Come on, Scotty," urged Fly.

"What do you think, Horse?" asked Scotty.

"I don't know."

"Ah, come on," said Bullock.

"I don't think we should," said Horse. "It aint right."

"You're either with us or against us," said Snake with a mean look in his eye. "If you're not with us then get on ya horse and go."

Horse looked around to everyone in turn, "I'll go," and mounted his horse.

"You'll go south," insisted Bullock. I don't want them stinking camel herders to know we're here."

"I got ya, Bullock. You don't need to tell me anything," replied Horse. "You should change your mind, Scotty, before it's too late."

"Shut your mouth, Horse!" said Snake

With that said Horse turned away from Scotty and leapt upon his horse before heading away from the scene, Scotty looking to the ground and then to Bullock.

"You're either in or out," said Bullock. "What's it going to be?"

Bullock had made up his mind. His father had told him all, spared no insult, regardless of how small.

Bullock had grown tired of the thievery, the Afghans taking the work from them all, the Afghans conducting the work at a cheaper rate and handling their camels to conduct the tasks with seemingly great ease and without infliction. Regardless of the fact that the Afghans were answering the call from settlers, mines and explorers, the young and old men of the Australian bush could simply not come to terms with the loss of employment.

There was no word of forgiveness from the white man, no word of thanks. The Afghans had insulted the colonists... they didn't drink alcohol, failed to consume the luxuries and amenities offered by the white man, and above all, spent very little of what they earned; and when money was spent it was mostly in stores run by other Afghan men or hawkers of a similar caste.

"I'm in," said Scotty after a little silence.

"That's great, Scotty," said Fly with a smile, "fantastic," but Scotty simply frowned as Snake turned to edge his way towards the lip of the creek line, to see for himself how the cameleers had progressed.

## CHAPTER FORTY-FOUR

Bullock shuffled up and lay beside Scotty.

And what was about to unfold was but the tip of the iceberg and only the beginning in regards to the dissatisfaction to be displayed by colonists for the contracts between the cameleers and pastoralists, for the hatred against these great men was about to get worse.

Bullock had failed to realise that it was in the 1860s that many camels and their handlers were imported into the country to aid in the widening of Australian occupied territory, discovering more and more, far and wide. It was all an exercise of the great awakening where the laying of the telegraph from Port Augusta to Darwin was but pittance to the actual advantages to be won from the land over the decades to come.

But regardless of Bullock's knowledge on history, regardless of how much he actually knew about these men, the Afghans had to be put into their place and shown once and for all who was boss.

But there was something else that infuriated the boys even more than words could express and it was a story that had been passed onto them from their fathers, a story which could not be tolerated.

Bullock told Scotty, as he laid there, the story.

This Afghan that they saw before them, as advised by a friend when they were seen bypassing Mulka far and wide, was a villain.

Their eyes looked upon the jemadar and his string through

branches and over spinifex. He was surely the one; he looked the same, even from that distance... that grin, the way in which his mouth was present upon his face without a move, steadfast in a grimace of never-ending hatred for whomever he met.

It was said that he and several others had been spotted at one time, somewhere along this very track, drinking water from a small waterhole during a time when water was scarcer than any other. But that wasn't the crime, oh no. The crime was the fact that it was time for prayer and the Afghans, with little concern for others that might pass that way, took their shoes and socks off to wash their feet – to wash in the only water for miles around. This act simply could not be tolerated.

"That's one of many stories I know," said Bullock. "It has to be stopped. I can't take any more."

Scotty looked into his friend's eyes, not really knowing him at all.

"Do you think he deserves to die?" asked Scotty.

"I do," said Bullock, "for all he's done, for all his grievances against us."

Snake appeared beside them, "Come on; you ready or what? Get back here so we can spread out proper."

The four congregated in the low ground behind the bush and prepared themselves as best they could, Snake and Bullock taking position so as to be closest to the string when it passed them by.

## CHAPTER FORTY-FIVE

Four men, as seen through their own eyes; four boys as seen through those of their parents. They had settled into wait and watched the caravan of 14 camels and three cameleers draw ever closer.

Bullock thought it strange that so many cameleers should be required to accompany so few camels and surmised that they were 'three' simply to provide one-another company during the long treks across the country. He couldn't help but briefly consider the work that they did, the time they sacrificed in order to bring a little luxury to the lives of settlers. It was all for nothing, for the ideas were quickly syphoned through what intellect he had and put to waste like common garbage, and his eyes fell to the barrel of his rifle.

He'd never killed a man before but the hatred within him was sure to put him to ease, just for a moment, long enough to pull the trigger and see a man die.

Snake was of dissimilar view and only thought of how badly these cameleers had been towards him and those of the past, of all he knew of their callous ways to deny his family the ability to earn good money and put food on the table.

For Snake the killing would come easily and his only wish was that the cameleers were riding upon a camel so that when the shots were fired the dead would have further to fall, toppled from their high stations upon their pets.

Questions rose within Scotty, he wondered about the effects of the rifles. He'd seen rabbits and dingoes killed sure enough, but never a man. Did a man bleed the same as a rabbit? Did a man squirm upon the ground in the same dying fashion; or did he yelp like a wounded dog? But last of all he considered what they were about to do and couldn't help but have second thoughts, wondering whether two rifles would be enough. He picked up a couple of large rocks to appease his need for security.

Fly had a smile upon his face as he looked out upon the approaching string but quickly lost all feeling of excitement when he looked over and towards Bullock, the menacing look in his friend's eyes leaving no doubt at all as to what was about to be delivered.

The cameleers had no names to the young men but their features were enough to distinguish one from another.

Nak was to the front as usual, leading Chocolate ever closer to the torment that was about to befall them all, with Shir at the rear and Abdul to the centre as usual. Nak was thinking of the love he held for Saki and the need to hold her in his arms, as well as the string which he would have to increase in number as soon as the opportunity presented itself. It was all possible that Faiz Mahomet would provide him with a few animals to help in the bad times ahead.

Shir considered his wife, for he missed her immensely, the Aboriginal woman that was different from the rest. There was simply no way that you could compare her to the others that were seen during his treks across the desert. He could see Arika smiling down upon him from within the comfort of their bed, their eyes locked in unison before making good the opportunity to make love once more.

As for Abdul, he was by far different than the other two. It wasn't from lack of experience or work ethic when it came down to operating strings out of Marree but simply that he was married to a wife who was still in Afghanistan and had children. For him there was no other place on earth but his home... and he

*Afghan*

had left it to make his fortune.

## CHAPTER FORTY-SIX

Nak frowned upon the behaviour he was now witnessing, Chocolate becoming unsettled and looking off into the bush upon the highest portion of high ground to their left, a small lip of extended ground that fell into a dry creek bed.

Nak thought that a snake might be nearby and scoured the area with his eyes, looking rather intently for any sign of reptilian life within the spinifex around.

"What is it?" asked Abdul.

"I'm not sure," replied Nak. "Chocolate senses something... I'm not sure."

Nak pulled down hard upon the harness of Chocolate and at that moment the unmistakable sound of a rifle shot pierced the air.

"My god!" yelled Abdul as he took to the ground, forgetting his finger for the moment but brought quickly back to reality as he fell with all his weight upon it, releasing his hold on the camel.

Nak too, was quick to find comfort in security and within a matter of several seconds; and by the time the second shot rang out he had his own rifle pulled from hiding.

"Shir," yelled Nak, seeing Abdul laying flat upon the ground, but unsure of Shir's safety. "Shir; are you okay?"

There was no answer and so Abdul chanced a look in his direction, seeing the prostrate form of his friend lying upon the ground.

The four Australian boys then broke from hiding and raced

down towards the three cameleers, unsure whether or not any of them had been hit fatally with the firing of their rifles. Bullock took a brief look towards Snake, who having fired a little slow for his liking, was making up for his poor showing by being the first of them to reach the string of fourteen camels.

Snake's eye fell upon Shir as he lashed out with a knife and cut in one smooth action the string attached from nose peg to camel. The kitchen camel simply pulled away in the build-up of panic from rifle shot to screaming assailants. All along the line camels reared their heads, some pegs breaking loose from camels and others requiring a little aid from a sharp knife.

Snake looked down again upon Shir and saw blood oozing from his back, lying there flat, dead as an autumn leaf, the colour of death spreading across the cameleer's back.

Abdul quickly stood as Scotty and Fly swooped past him, one to either side and slashing at all manner of throng and leash, the camels bucking and pulling, groaning and racing away into the desert around them, all unrestricted by hobble.

Abdul hadn't yet seen Shir lying there with blood seeking from the exit wound upon his back, nor the seated form of Snake as the boy collapsed beside the dead man, a great surge of sorrow having burst the banks within him. Snake had killed a man, the first and last he wished to kill, and even then he found a momentary loss as to why it was so important to have killed this man, the cameleer with no name.

Fly grabbed hold of a camel, that quick as a flash bit him upon the hand. Fly pulled the hand back with the pain and fright of the bite but was quick to take revenge on the seemingly pathetic beast by thrusting his knife into the animal's neck.

Abdul hit the boy hard in the side of the leg, the pain of the hit destabilizing Fly who then fell upon the ground. Abdul rallied all his strength and pulled himself upon the fallen and for only the second time in his entire life lashed out with a closed fist.

Fly pulled his arms up to cover his face as he lay there until rescued from harm by his friend Scotty, who braced himself for the worse and tackled Abdul from the rear. With the pain of his amputated finger forgotten, Abdul needed to now contend with a surging fury of pain in the lower part of his back and he crumpled into a ball, screaming out for the world to hear.

Fly was upon his feet in seconds and prepared to escape with Scotty close behind.

Bullock, meanwhile, having forgotten to reload his rifle after the initial shot being fired, lashed out with the butt of his weapon which connected squarely upon the jaw of Nak. Nak fell heavily as Bullock went to work upon the camels' restraints, not noticing that Nak was quick to recover and pulled the rifle to him.

Nak got the weapon ready for firing and brought it into his shoulder but Bullock had since taken off between two camels and was currently unobserved. Fly fell within Nak's field of view and as the boy stood, Nak fired a single shot whereby the boy fell down dead in an instant, his mouth open to the world as his last breath ever was inhaled.

"NO!" yelled Scotty who went to his aid, tripped by Abdul and ended up with his face buried in the ground, his nose breaking in place upon his left cheek.

Snake shook the reality of the dead man beside him from his mind and looked out and over towards where the third rifle shot was heard. He saw his friend, Fly, fall hard upon the ground and knew, right then and there, that Fly was dead.

## CHAPTER FORTY-SEVEN

Horse heard the first of the rifle shots in the distance far behind him and realising that the attack had commenced couldn't help thinking that he should have done more in preventing the massacre of the three cameleers.

Suddenly, on hearing the second shot, he pulled upon the reins of his horse that came to a dead stop, neither fidgeting nor having a care in the world as Horse considered what should be done.

The third shot rang out and Horse turned the head of the beast he was riding and headed off back towards where his friends had been left to their own vices of evil doing.

Horse was overcome with different emotions and wasn't entirely sure which emotion should be adhered to and which should be discarded. The fighting within himself was little more than the question of good over bad. He understood full well that the idea of Bullocks, which he so easily implanted within the others, was to cause as much disarray as possible, scattering the camels to the four winds. The death of the cameleers was simply a bonus, as far as Bullock was concerned, and whether one died or all, it mattered little to him.

Horse knew of their plan to escape to the south, hence creating a little confusion before heading back into Mulka at a later date, and before any suspicion as to their involvement could be readily formulated. If he continued in the direction he was heading in he was sure to come into contact with them.

He wasn't entirely sure why he was returning but he felt as

though something had gone wrong. It was the third shot... it somehow sounded different than the others. From so far away from the action he was sure that he could hear a difference between the third and the first two shots being fired.

He was trotting at a reasonable speed when he'd reached the point just half way between where he was and the site that Bullock had chosen for delivering his mayhem. He could make out a little noise not so very far ahead when he realised what it was.

"Bullock," said Horse, "is that you?"

Bullock lifted his head from behind some brush followed by the head of Snake.

Horse dismounted and walked over to where they were crouched, himself crouching as he approached in fear of being seen by any prying eyes. He could see that both were filled with grief, Snake more than Bullock.

Horse knelt down beside the other two.

"Where's Fly and Scotty?" he asked

The silence that followed was clear, but clarity askew.

"Were they caught?" asked Horse.

Bullock looked him in the eye, "Scotty was captured."

"And Fly?"

"He's dead," said Snake flatly but decisively.

"We don't know that for sure," said Bullock with his rifle in hand.

"I saw him," said Snake, "before I got away," and looked to Horse.

"Where's your rifle?" asked Horse.

"He left it behind," said Bullock. "Now they have two—."

Snake punched Bullock in the face before being set upon by Horse.

"That's enough; no more!" insisted Horse as he got between the pair. "I'm more concerned about Fly and Scotty."

"It's no good," insisted Snake. "Fly is dead; I know it. When I heard the third shot fired I looked up and saw Fly fall. Scotty fell down after but I think he's okay."

"So what happened to your rifle?" asked Horse.

"I guess I dropped it."

"Dropped it!" repeated Bullock sarcastically.

"Enough," stabbed Horse. "We gotta think now. We can't just leave Scotty there with those men."

"I don't think I can do any more," said Snake. "I feel sick inside," and the look upon his face was sincere.

"You should have thought about that earlier," said Horse. "But now it's too late and we have to help."

"I still got my rifle," said Bullock.

"I don't know," said Horse. "They have two, we have one."

"We'll shoot first and ask later."

"This isn't funny, Bullock," spat Snake.

"No one said it was," said Bullock. "We have to go in armed, we have no choice now."

"You're right," said Horse. "I don't think we have a choice."

Snake looked up dismayed and sad, feeling the horrors of his deed growing within him, "I killed one of them."

"Don't feel guilty, Snake," said Bullock. "They got one of us, too. I think we should finish this and get back to Mulka."

"He's right," agreed Horse, looking into Snake's eyes. "We have to save Scotty. Where are your horses?"

"We don't have them."

"Then we'll have to get them back, too," concluded Horse needlessly.

## CHAPTER FORTY-EIGHT

Shir had been laid in a blanket and placed in the shade of one of the trees aligning the dry creek bed, a swarm of flies trying their luck at gaining entry to the dead man in order to lay their eggs.

"The flies I hate the worse," said Nak. "Forever on our backs and in our eyes and ears; and now poor Shir is dead and they want some of him."

"What shall we do now?" asked Abdul of the jemadar.

Nak looked over to where the dead boy, Fly, was laying, infested with flies, Nak having done nothing to prevent the onslaught from taking place for he felt that the boy deserved all he received.

"Let the maggots have their feast upon his rotting carcass," said Nak and then he looked to the other, tied to the base of a tree and in easy vision of his dead friend. "What name you?"

Scotty didn't answer at first; he had a broken nose and it was bruised and bloody, he also had two black eyes where he'd been hit uncontrollably by Nak earlier on.

Nak stood up and hurried over to him, but before he could lash out with a kick to the boy's body he screamed out and curled into a ball as best he could, "SCOTTY!" The kick didn't come and Scotty returned to his original position, shaking from his ordeal. "My name is Scotty."

"You friend coward, run quick, much far away now," said Nak as he tried to break the boy. "Horse now mine, you nothing. I get pretty good money of horse."

"I don't think he cares," pointed out Abdul who fell silent

briefly and then asked the question upon his mind. "What are we to do now?"

"We'll have to tell the police, and hand the boy into the authorities," answered Nak. "I don't see any other alternative. I don't exactly trust the police but what choice do we have. We can't let the boy go because he'll tell lies and we could end up being convicted of murder, but with the boy in custody, along with the horses, I think we can fairly well sell our story of self-defence."

"Don't you think we should cover the boy's body before the maggots eat too much? The police won't take kindly to us leaving him to be eaten like this. His parents will take unkindly—"

"I don't care, Abdul," interrupted Nak. "The people here can think what they like. I'm sick to death of them all. Even those we serve have condemned our beliefs by smuggling bacon upon the loads we carry. None of them can be trusted."

"When will we leave?"

"Tomorrow morning," said Nak. "We'll take the few camels we have along with the horses. The horses can be used to carry the dead; the prisoner we'll make walk for a while but let him ride later, when he's tired... I want to get to Marree as quickly as possible."

"What about the other camels; the lost?"

"They'll have to stay lost. We have to move quickly. Maybe we can come back for them later."

"In that case, wouldn't it be best to leave the wool here; there's hardly enough to worry about?"

"You're right," said Nak. "I'll consider it tonight."

"You realise that the other boys might come back, and from my recollection they still have a rifle."

"We have two," said Nak and then thought of the wool. "We won't get far now, anyway. We have just three camels with us and four horses. We have no stores to speak of except a little water; my Koran is gone along with our prayer mats. We have nothing left. Help me, Abdul. We'll secure the camels in the creek bed beside the horses. Scotty can stay where he is for the night and suffer the cold. Get a fire going.

"And the others?"

"We'll maintain watch, just like when in the army. We can set up a small watching post and watch for the others, and I wish good visuals to be maintained with the rising of the sun. If they approach the fire then they must be shot; we can't afford to be caught unaware."

"They have the advantage," said Abdul knowingly.

"Yes, but we have a prisoner and two rifles."

"You know... I'm not afraid to die, just concerned for my family back at home," said Abdul. "They'll never know what happened to me. I just think it's more kind for them to know what I did here and that I just didn't abandon them."

"Your wife loves you, Abdul. She'll not think unkindly."

"And what about you, Nak? Are you afraid to die?"

"There is life after death, dear friend. I will be thirty-two years old for eternity and have seventy-two virgins to appease my every need. What more could a man ask from heaven?" and he thought then of Saki.

"It's good for you," said Abdul, endeavouring to make a joke. "You are forty-two at present and so get a good deal if you die; I'm only twenty-three at present, so gain nine years."

"And you are married," said Nak. "That will have an effect on your ability to enjoy seventy-two virgins."

Abdul smiled, "You're right," he said, "It's too many for me. Maybe I'll give you some of mine."

"My dear friend, Abdul, even seventy-two virgins is too good to wish for, any more and I'll die a second death."

## CHAPTER FORTY-NINE

Snake led the way with Bullock close behind with Horse leading his horse on foot.

The advance was suddenly brought to a temporary close as Snake put up a hand to halt those behind, seeing something to his front that wasn't particularly of any great surprise.

"What is it? What do you see?" asked Bullock.

"Another camel."

Bullock lifted his rifle into his shoulder and looked down the sights on seeing the animal, his head held low and teeth raking at the spinifex that it had found.

Horse approached from behind and slammed his palm down upon the barrel of the rifle, knocking the sight picture from Bullock's grasp, unsettling his friend who was hiding his nervousness of the entire situation from the other two, "Don't be foolish; idiot."

"Damn; that hurt," said Bullock as he looked at Horse. "I've got a good mind to smash your face in."

"Why don't you?"

"Because it's what the cameleers want," intruded Snake. "They'd love for you to give our position away."

"No shooting, Bullock," said Horse.

"I got a better idea," said Snake and headed off slowly towards the camel after taking an axe handle from Horse's gear.

"What are you doing?" asked Horse.

"Do you want these camels to fester the land you call home?" questioned Snake and the as he turned to his task whispered, "you damn fool."

Snake approached the camel as the other two watched on, the sun slowly disappearing below the horizon with the camel eating what he'd found, food for the taking, now at his disposal.

He crept ever closer, more slowly as he closed the gap, to the impatience of the other two. The camel appeared to ignore Snake's presence as he moved around to the rear and moved ever closer. He moved his hands around the axe handle and took a good grip. Once satisfied and close enough he swung hard and low, the camel's leg breaking instantly.

The noise that erupted from within the camel was so loud and disgustingly horrific that Horse covered his eyes beneath is palms and Bullock simply watched on open-mouthed as Snake moved up to the camel laying upon the ground in great agony and proceeded to smash its head in until the head of the axe handle was so covered in membranes and blood that it was hardly recognizable.

Bullock approached Snake, "Come on, Snake, that's enough," he pleaded. "It's dead now; give it a rest will ya."

Snake stopped pounded down upon the carcass, "I'm sick of these bloody animals. Good for nothing is what they are, taking what work is available away from me and me dad."

"It's not just you," said Horse as he drew alongside, looking down upon the blood and the brain of the camel. "We all suffer."

"And now it's time they suffered," said Snake. "We'll wait till it gets dark; they'll have to light a fire sooner or later: won't they?"

"I'd sure hope so," said Horse, "otherwise poor old Scotty's going to have a terrible night."

"Well, let's see if we can't help him out a little," said Snake. "Come on, let's get out of here; this camel stinks."

## CHAPTER FIFTY

The sky above was a brilliant dark blue, a darkness never forgotten, and a peaceful reminder that man was a small part of a larger picture. Abdul didn't know much about the heavens, other than what he'd read in the Koran, but knew enough to find his way around at night.

He was sitting next to a large bush and facing towards where the campfire burnt low and bright, the brightness evaporating into the night and extinguishing itself, the edge between light and dark fairly distinct.

The cold of the night was starting to take effect upon him but he had a warm blanket wrapped around his thin form, the flesh of his hands the only thing not protected as they held on tightly to the rifle in his lap.

Abdul was content to sit where he was for half the night; to await the boys he knew would return sooner or later. He had both rifles with him, both with a round of ammunition up the spout and ready to fire.

Nak rolled over in his sleep and the boy, Scotty, was stretched out from the tree, his feet seeking as much warmth as possible. He'd had a gag placed over his mouth prior to the cameleers preparing for the night so that the boy wouldn't be able to alert his friends of the predicament when they came calling, for a second bed roll had been placed out beside the fire to look as though it contained another person; and in fact it did. The dead man, Shir, was placed beside the fire to trick the other boys into believing that both men were asleep.

Abdul cocked his head a little having heard something off in the distance. He couldn't be sure but he was sure that he'd heard a stick being trodden underfoot. He strained his ears, leaning his head a little to the side in order to gain better hearing. A horse could be heard far, far away and this was followed by the sighting of a silhouette, a single figure.

Someone was approaching and with much stealth, crouched a little to help hide his presence from view.

Abdul looked over towards where Scotty was lying and knew immediately that he had fallen asleep, otherwise he'd be thrashing about to alert the one that was near.

Another two figures then appeared out of nowhere and the first beams of light from the fire revealed the front figure. He wasn't carrying a rifle and so one of the others held that. They were a little too close for comfort. If Nak was to stir or jump up once the shooting had commenced then he was in great risk of being shot himself.

Abdul decided then and there to do what he must do. He had sworn unto himself to treat everyone the same, not to do unto one that he did not expect to have done to him. And so this was the reality of his promise to himself, for there was a rifle amongst the three and although it had not been revealed just yet, it was still there and very dangerous.

Abdul lifted his rifle and without a shadow of a doubt crossing his mind, and with the fury of the death of Shir behind him, squeezed the trigger of the rifle as he had been taught back in Afghanistan.

The loud firing of the rifle was enough to wake the devil, not to mention Scotty and Nak.

The shot was a success and Snake fell down hard, wounded heavily in the stomach, a wound from which he would not recover. A heavy gasp for air erupted from within him.

Nak sprang to his feet at the same time that Bullock panicked and fired his rifle, having not taken good aim like his counterpart, the shot flying not so far from its proposed point of aim and hit Abdul in the right shoulder.

The pain was instantaneous but remarkably held at bay, for the reality of the situation was overpowering to say the least.

Abdul had the second rifle in is hand with swift ease and steadiness. He pulled the trigger this time, anxious to get the shot off, and with as much luck as can be afforded him the shot hit Bullock square in the head, killing him instantly. Bullock's body fell like a sack of spuds upon the ground, not a sound coming from him other than the thud as he fell.

Horse raced over to where Bullock had fallen, his mind clear and decisive, understanding fully the predicament he and his friends were in. He picked the rifle up and searched quickly for the ammunition that Bullock carried.

The scene was alive with men and boys moving around, gasps of pain and grunts of effort being heard, but not a single word, sentence or phrase was uttered in those few seconds that had led to the growing misery that surrounded them all.

Nak was now upon his feet and raced towards Horse only to be confronted by Snake who unselfishly kicked out with much pain being suffered in his gut, the sheer effort enough to tax him hard of all his energy.

The bleeding of Snake was largely internal and the pain just then surfaced like a volcano bursting its banks: not only was the larva now spouting from the top but it was forcing great pressure on his inside. Snake gasped for air just then, drawing on every effort to take another breath, but no breath came. Snake died, the last fragments of thought rushing through his mind being those of his family at home. He could see the face of his mother gently fade from memory as his mind went blank once and for all.

Nak fell hard upon the ground, a blade of spinifex forced into his eye. The shock of the fall and the pain of the spinifex that had penetrated the eye was enough to keep Nak occupied whilst Horse quickly found some ammunition and loaded the rifle. He brought the stock into his shoulder and shot at comparatively point-blank range the body mass of Nak.

Nak's stirring fell silent. The range from firer-to-target had seen to Nak's death as surely as the penetration of the spinifex had seen to the pain within his eye.

Abdul saw all of this but couldn't tell who was alive, who was dead, or who was down and out of the fight. It was now that the pain in his arm commenced to build slightly. He fumbled around for what he had placed beside his knee and reloaded the first rifle. He brought the weapon up into his shoulder as best he could with the injury he'd sustained and awaited his next opportunity, to fire the weapon at the strongest target, for it was better to deal with a wounded enemy opposed to a live one.

Horse threw the rifle to the ground at that moment, spurred on by several emotional traits. He could see Scotty over by the tree as he kicked and rolled upon the ground, trying to draw his friend's attention, but the largest of Horse's weaknesses was the fact that he'd just shot a man for no other reason than that surrounding his prejudice.

Horse was in a flurry, unsure what he should do and whether or not he should do it, and before he realised what was happening he found himself kneeling beside Scotty with a knife in his hand and cutting away at his bonds.

Abdul couldn't believe the stupidity of the boy and how he'd simply raced up to his friend. Such comradeship was hard to find in men. These whites were not much different than he, but he would not have killed for the sake of killing. He, Abdul, would not have shot at defenceless cameleers as they made their way from town to town to try and earn a little money for their hungry children. And so, without further thought, he squeezed the trigger and killed the one that Horse was trying to save. Abdul shot Scotty, the wounded, to let the healthy live, to give the one with courage that last opportunity to save himself in the face of his honour and courage.

Horse heard the shot fired and in the light of the campfire saw the blood erupt from Scotty's head. Horse knew then and there that he was up against men who had dealt with weapons before, and had killed in their past. Horse didn't wish to be a statistic and was quickly brought back to reality.

"You go," shouted Abdul. "You go long way, no come back. You got horse, you take and go home. Me forget quick. Me not care. You live, me live; we both live. You know what meaning is?"

"Yes," replied Horse. "I know what you mean."

Horse looked down into the closed eyes of his friend. Of the five he was the only one left alive. "You've killed four of my friends. That'll be hard to live with."

"Alive is good, dead is bad," lectured Abdul. "You go and me go. We both go."

"Yes," said Horse as he stood, sheathing his knife. "We both go." Horse turned and commenced to move away. He stumbled to a stop. "Thank you," he said and continued on his way.

"Okay," said Abdul. "You do thing, one more. You make horse speak, me know you gone."

"Yes; yes, okay," said Horse, understanding full well that Abdul wished to ensure that he, Horse, was actually out of range and not to return for vengeance. "But I'll be back tomorrow, to get my friends. If you are still here then I'll not make any promises."

Abdul nodded but it wasn't seen as Horse disappeared into the desert.

## CHAPTER FIFTY-ONE

Abdul was on foot now and staggering a little as he made his way south. He'd patched his wound up as best he could but wished to be on his way and in the company of his new friends at Marree.

He'd left the bodies of the whites behind but his friends were with him. Nak and Shir were strapped to two of the camels in the string and the third carried nothing but the last of the water that he had. The thought of riding upon the camel hadn't even entered his mind; such was the decay of his normality. His thinking was askew and thoughts mostly of home. This was his first real job and might well be his last.

As he continued towards Marree, the camels knowing the way as much as he, he considered the two corpses that he carried.

Nak was a good jemadar and little was known about his personal life. He never spoke much on his feelings of love and loneliness. Shir on the other hand couldn't shut up when it came to speaking of his wife and the love he felt for her; it was enough to make him ill with home-sickness.

Nak Kadir was from Kabul, single and aged forty-two. Shir Adji was from Karachi, married to Arika; Shir was thirty-three and his wife just sixteen. He would remember them, remember them always.

The blistering heat of the day continued to build as he made progress. His water was gone and he had no food. With little experience of survival in this new country, and with the weight of keeping clear of any settlers, Europeans, colonists, and the like – although they were all the same when it came down to it – he was starting to feel extremely weary.

He looked down upon the ground as he walked, unable to see his shadow for the sun was high in the sky. He'd had no sleep the night before and had suffered badly over the past week or more. There was so much that he'd been exposed to that he wasn't sure if it was all reality or simply a dream.

He continued on for several more hours and before long he tripped upon a small rock that was half buried in the track, the loss of blood from his shoulder wound having taken its toll upon him. He fell silently and quickly upon the ground and darkness came once more.

## CHAPTER FIFTY-TWO

The jolting of the wagon woke Abdul up and as he stirred a familiar voice echoed in his ear.

"Ah, praise the good lord that you have risen," said Brother Ernest. "You've been in and out of your daze for a few days now. How do you feel?"

Abdul understood enough of what was said but still had a lot of blurriness to contend with. He rubbed at his eyes and was suddenly reminded of the pain in his shoulder.

"Ah; I fixed that as best I could," said Ernest who had moved from walking beside his beasts of burden to having taken a seat upon the wagon to more readily view Abdul. "I stopped the bleeding, but it took some time."

"Where we go?" asked Abdul.

"I found you beside the track, unconscious. I was on my way to Killalpinanna but have decided to turn about and take you to Marree. It's the least I can do for a religious man, even if it goes against the grain."

"Where friend?"

"What friend? Ah; you mean the others? I don't know. You know; I thought it was strange that they should leave you alone like that. Did one of them shoot you?"

"No. You no see friends? They dead."

"Are they dead? I don't know," said Ernest slightly confused.

"No, no. Not meaning. Friend is dead; you find; you see them and camels?" asked Abdul sparingly and with a little difficulty.

Ernest handed Abdul a water canteen, "Here, have a drink,"

he offered. "No, I didn't see anyone. No camels, no friends. Just you; and lucky I came across you when I did otherwise you'd be dead."

Abdul thought on the matter and came to the only conclusion possible at present. Nak and Shir were strapped to the camels. The camels must have taken off into the desert after he'd collapsed. They were lost forever upon the backs of the camels that carried them.

"We shouldn't be long into Marree," said Ernest. "You'll have to report this to the police."

Abdul considered what was said. This was a problem which just wouldn't go away easily. Without the bodies of Nak and Shir he had little to tell the police. Other than a few people that had seen him the day before their departure to the homestead, and the two Aboriginal boys, whose names now escaped him, no one really knew of him. The circumstances of his being shot could not really be confirmed or proved. The white boy, on the other hand, he could say what he wished and would be believed.

Maybe it was time to let sleeping ghosts lie and say nothing of what had happened. Maybe he should try and return to Afghanistan whilst he had the chance.

"No," said Abdul

"No!" said Ernest. "Well, it's not my place to force it upon you, after all you were found alone. It seems to me that justice should be delivered to those that left you there to die."

"I forgive, and forget," but Abdul wasn't so sure that he could ever forget the ordeal he'd suffered.

"I'll take you to the Ghantown then," offered Ernest. "Would you like that? I have to do something, I can't just simply, 'not' help a man in need."

Abdul smiled then and looked up at the man known as Brother Ernest Jacob.

"You good friend," said Abdul. "You good man this place. Me

never forget."

Ernest simply smiled and turned his eyes again upon the track to his front as he continued on across the wilderness.

Abdul considered his final option. He'd return home to his family in Afghanistan. Life in Australia was simply too hard.

And with reflection upon his wife and children at home overpowering the thoughts of Nak and Shir, he smiled a heavenly smile and thanked God for his being allowed to survive; for what would he do with seventy-two virgins?